ELUSIVE QUARRY

B. COMFORT

ELUSIVE QUARRY

A Foul Play Press Book

The Countryman Press, Inc.
Woodstock, Vermont

ISBN 0-88150-370-3

Published by Foul Play Press,
a division of The Countryman Press
PO Box 175, Woodstock, Vermont 05091-0175.
Distributed by W.W. Norton & Company, Inc.
500 Fifth Avenue
New York, NY 10110

Cover design and illustration by David Powell

Printed in the United States of America
10 9 8 7 6 5 4 3 2 1

AUTHOR'S ACKNOWLEDGMENT

Without Bill Markcrow's help, everything about a
quarry would certainly have been elusive.

One

I was in a lovely state of limbo halfway between consciousness and sleep. Stretched out on a slab of slate, my old carcass warmed by the autumn sun, I was lulled by the sound of my pug's gentle snore. Bees buzzed in a patch of hawkweed. I was roused by the clarion sound of a yodel.

Sophie, hands cupped around her mouth, repeated her call. Lulu responded by leaping into her arms.

"Dear girl," I said, sitting up, "we've never discussed this accomplishment of yours. Do they yodel in Hawaii? Isn't it a little tropical there for edelweiss, lederhosen, and all that?"

My cousin Marion, who lived in Maui, had acquired my lovely young friend as a stepdaughter when she married Sophie's father ten years ago. Sophie described me as her aunt and I loved claiming her as my niece.

"I learned to yodel in Girl Scouts. Sounds great echoing over the Pali."

Today was the day, I thought. I should say: Stop. Stand right there. Don't move. I'll go get my paints and paint what we used to call, half a century ago, a mudhead: a model painted against a bright background with broad strokes of a palette knife.

Sophie looked more hoyden than glamour girl today. Her tall slim figure and honey-colored hair were topped with a white painter's cap worn backwards. I hate those damned hats, but the white in shadow was beautiful. Her gray-green eyes were framed by long lashes and dark eyebrows that almost met in the middle. One straight firm stroke of the palette knife would do for her nose and a dab of crimson and cadmium yellow might catch the glow of her cheeks. A long slash of white would be required for her smile.

Sophie said her teeth were her secret weapon. She could intimidate the enemy by threatening to bite them. The rest of her costume was standard Sophie—a ragged T-shirt, very short cut-off jeans, and sneakers with holes in the toes.

I pinched my nostrils. "I know what you've been doing."

"Yeah. Have yet to learn how to clean out the barn without smelling like eau de goat. I'm getting ready for the Thetford Fair."

Sophie's small herd of cashmere goats had played a lively role in my life ever since she acquired them last year. I offered to help her with the grooming. The beasts loved to be brushed. Van Goat, her prize buck, had become so arrogant and vain that the only way to approach him was with a brush in hand.

"The show's not for another week. And thanks, I will need help."

She sat down beside me, licked her finger, and rubbed a circle on the bench. "Slate, isn't it?"

"Vermont slate, yes."

"I've been meaning to tell you, Tish. I met this fabulous guy a while back and you won't believe this. He's in slate."

"Entombed?"

"Oh, come on. In the business. He, like, runs a mine, or a quarry or whatever. You know—sells slate."

"Is he a miner?"

"No. He owns the place. He inherited it."

"Is he a geologist?"

"Nope. He's learning the business from the bottom up. And when I say bottom, that means something. He says the quarry is like the Grand Canyon."

I wondered if it was the same quarry that I went to with my late husband Doug. The memory brought to mind the conical piles of slate waste that sprang out of the landscape like chunky gray pyramids. I remembered us choosing the color of slate and the shape we wanted for a coffee table top, for the back steps, and for the bench we sat on.

"Have you been there, wherever it is?" I asked.

"Poultney. Not yet. Been too busy with the goats. How about tomorrow? Do you want to go with me?"

"Where are we going tomorrow?"

Sophie and Lulu both dashed toward the tall old man who watched with disgust as his load of groceries slid out of the bottom of his brown paper bag and rolled onto the grass.

"Here I try to make the world a better place for unborn millions by using paper bags and they put a wet head of lettuce in the bottom of this goddamned thing.

"I was just coming to invite you ladies for dinner tonight. Hey!" he yelled at Lulu, who was trying to open a butcher's package. "Not now, you vulture. You can have the leftovers later. Well?" He opened his brown hands, palms as taut as stretched parchment, and placed them on his nonexistent hips. "You both seem to be able to contain your enthusiasm. Sophie?"

9

Sophie sat on the grass cross-legged, with Lulu in her lap, reading the label on a can of kidney beans. "Let's see— hmmmm—tonight. I'm trying to visualize my engagement calendar. Is it Saturday or Sunday? Hmmmmm."

"I have some bait, Sophie. Maybe a little senior for you, but a nice fella. Wants to buy my land on the mountain."

"I hope you told him to stand in line. What's his name?"

"Gray Graham. Or maybe it's Graham Gray."

"Married?"

"Have no idea. But I'm not inviting you to mate—just eat."

"Sophie tells me she has a new playmate. What's his name?"

"Sid. Sid Colt," Sophie answered. "You'll hate him, Hilary." Sophie smiled at Hilary, who was lining up groceries on a windowsill. "What I mean is you'll hate him at first. He's given to wearing loose homespuns and sandals."

"Oh, God."

My octogenarian neighbor and best friend Hilary Oats looked as though he should be handing his lance and helmet to a servant or adjusting his bagpipe strap across his square bony shoulders or even raising his hand to still the roar of the crowd. He sighed as he examined a bruised peach.

"Now wait a minute, Hil. Sid's no spaceshot. He's a businessman. Nothing fuzzy. You'll see. He's thinking of buying in Lofton, too."

Hilary found all of Sophie's playmates and suitors unqualified. He adored my gregarious niece and tried with warriorlike determination to screen the candidates for her attention, with no success.

Her last wild romance had been a disaster but left her happily unscathed. I shared Hilary's concern but lacked the sensibilities of a *dueña*. I figured, since Sophie is a grown woman with reasonably good sense, her zest for life was bound to get her in trouble from time to time. But unlike Hilary, I thought her choice of friends and conduct was her own business. She was quick on her feet and was blessed with the resilience of youth. Memories of my own youth made me wince—but I'd made it and expected the same agility of Sophie. As I occasionally reminded Hilary, women are tough.

Sophie got up and straightened the collar of Hilary's polo shirt. "I'd love to come for dinner tonight. Give me a buzz if you need a sous-chef." She wiggled her fingers at me. "We'll talk about tomorrow tonight."

Hilary held up a package of ladyfingers with his pinky raised. "Got any exotic Asian teas? I want to get in the mood for that crazy girl's next lothario."

"Oh relax, Hil. You're obsessed. Did you know that? If you have to be so damned Victorian, why don't you think of Sophie's men as trolley cars passing by, one after the other. Better yet, don't think of them at all."

Hilary raised his eloquent eyebrows and, gathering the groceries, went into the kitchen.

Hilary thought of our kitchens as interchangeable. They certainly were different. Mine was a bright, tidy little oblong with a round table in the middle. Hilary's was a hopeless mess.

How he created his culinary marvels in his drunken-looking kitchen, I'll never know. Tangled electrical cords from every known gadget covered the counters like black-and-white spaghetti. There were racks of lethal knives and enough wooden mallets, spoons, and ladles to start a bonfire. The teetering stacks of cookbooks were not to be moved: They might be pressing the moisture out of an eggplant or flattening a crêpe. Dented colanders and charred pots and pans right out of hell swung above the stove. A string of garlic served as a light cord and the Yule season was recalled by a five-year-old wreath of bay leaves hanging in the window.

The kitchens were interchangeable in that it didn't matter whether Hilary unloaded the groceries at his house or mine; we both had a Scrabble board.

Once a month, Ruth, Hilary's long-suffering house cleaner, was allowed to clean the kitchen—a chore accompanied by words not fit for tender ears.

Hilary called through the kitchen window to ask if I preferred tea or coffee to go with the marmalade he had just bought.

"Either one. I'll be out in front."

Maybe there is a hotel on a lake in New Hampshire where people sit on the front porch rocking or in the South under the high ceiling of a plantation veranda. In any event, I think rocking chairs are severely underused. Except for the two substantial wicker rockers on my front porch. The soothing motion and the sound of the wooden rockers against the pine planks are the perfect accompaniment for drinking in the charm of Lofton.

I love the color of our village store across the street, which is a delicious mix of heavy cream and summer squash. The library, with its inviting bay window, seems to grow out of the patch of cadmium yellow lilies surrounding it. Our tiny post office is unfailingly described as cute or darling. The window boxes are crammed with marigolds that Charlie, the postmaster, says keep the mosquitoes away.

I have to turn my head to see the church. It is so close to my house that on summer days with the windows open I can sing along when the choir practices. The gas pump in front of Pete's cozy garage is barely visible through the maples. Only when the leaves fall can I see the rambling Lofton Inn from my front porch.

Lulu was purring in my lap like a kitten when Hilary appeared bearing our midmorning feast of coffee, toasted pita bread, and grapefruit marmalade. We munched and rocked and smiled at the typical Lofton scene. Myron, a huge Pyrenees dog, was fast asleep in the middle of the road and a brown Lab sitting beside him was lazily scratching summer's last flea bites.

"Move it, move it." A driver nearly tumbled out of his truck waving his fist at the dogs. After a luxurious stretch they rose, ambled over to the store, and collapsed on the porch.

The driver's patience was tried again as he maneuvered his boxy bread truck around a tricycle and two bikes abandoned in front of the post office.

I got up and busied myself breaking off the last of the frost-bitten geraniums.

"Hil—tonight, this gent who's interested in your property. What about him?"

"Nothing special. I want you to tell me what you think after you meet him."

"Did you hear Sophie say her slate man might be interested in buying, too?"

"Did she? Oh well. It's fun talking about it. But as you know, I'm in no rush to decide. There are so many options."

Two

Graham Gray might have been forty and I guessed he would look the same way forty years hence. He was so thin I could have painted him on a vertical half sheet of plywood. Tall as Graham was, Hilary, who complained about shrinking from his original six-feet-four, was taller.

The young man's pointed ears and circumflex eyebrows made me smile. I found it an appealing bony face.

"What a great place, sir. How long have you lived here?"

Hilary frowned. "How long have I lived here, Tish?"

Hilary had moved to Lofton at about the time Doug died, about fifteen years ago. He had sold his printing company in Rutland after his wife Alice died, and retired to this bungalow, which they had used as a summer camp.

Graham exclaimed over the three hefty ships' masts, still wearing their rigging, that were strategically placed around the living room. Most of us knew they literally held up the roof. A yard-sale-treasure painting of a barkentine in full sail was always askew, adding to the general impression of the passage of a gale-force wind. Just as the floor-to-ceiling stacks and shelves of books provided insulation from Lofty Mountain's cruel winter winds, the Oriental rugs, positioned like valances over the windows, served the same purpose when unrolled.

Graham lavished his greatest praise on Hilary's long coffee table, made out of piles of coffee table books.

"What'll it be?" Hilary flung open the door of an Oriental armoire. I always expected a shogun to leap out fully armed. "Scotch? Bourbon? Vodka? Vino?"

"Wine, please. Red if you have it, but please don't open a bottle on my account."

By the time he'd finished his sentence, Hil was opening a bottle of claret. "There you are." He dropped the cork in the scrap basket, held a wine glass up to the light, then handed it and the bottle to Graham. "All yours."

Lulu announced Sophie's arrival with a frenzy of sneezy barks. "Look." Sophie displayed two baskets of raspberries. "Would you believe it, this late in the season?"

With the briefest greeting to Graham, she and Hilary repaired to the kitchen, followed by Lulu, whom Hilary called his favorite garbage pail.

It didn't take long for me to warm up to Graham. I liked his enthusiasm and I found his air of bestowing a confidence when he spoke rather endearing.

No, he wasn't married. He'd been married but had been divorced in the last year. What does one hear? Don't make any important decisions the first year after a divorce.

Buying a hundred acres of prime land in Lofton was a pretty big decision. Plenty of people wanted Hilary's property. The Lofton Mountain ski group had been begging Hilary to sell it to them for years. Vermont conservation groups wanted him to turn its management over to them. The Vermont National Forest Service had offered to swap Hilary's hundred acres on the mountain which abutted on forest land for a hundred and twenty acres of land in Clement Hollow. He'd also considered giving the land to the town of Lofton to be kept forever wild, but the town was reluctant to accept the gift. They would prefer to see reasonable development that would increase the tax list.

Sophie reappeared shortly with a handful of flat silver and napkins. She plunked the load down at one end of the castle-sized refectory table.

"What a mess," she whispered. "How can he live like this?"

We pitched in and moved from the table a typewriter, a television set, a bushel basket of potatoes, folders, pads of paper, a jar of pencils, an empty wine bottle, and dozens of books. We left the row of green tomatoes ripening on a woolly winter scarf which was being shared by Hilary's cat, Vanessa.

"Well, I wondered where you were hiding." Sophie hugged the exotic café-au-lait creature and carried her over to the couch. She patted the cushion beside her and smiled at Graham. "Come talk to me. Sorry to be so rude, but the minute I come in, Hilary always has some urgent job for me to do in the kitchen. I just made some béarnaise sauce for the steak."

I took over the table-setting job and had a chance to look at Sophie's transformation. Smashing was the word. On top of dark crinkly slacks she wore a lemon yellow silk blouse. Her hair glistened and her big round earrings looked just right. I wondered if they were the kind that served as condom cases.

I realize that to many of the young, sex is no more important than a handshake—but I'm just enough of a romantic to hope that it isn't always the case.

"What did you say?" I realized I was getting into a bad habit of drifting off on my own miasmic cloud when I was supposed to be part of a group.

"Five places, Tish, not four," Sophie said. "My friend Sid's coming."

"You've told Hil?"

"Yup. Called him earlier. Guess he forgot to tell you."

What fun, I thought. A leftover hippie and upright, conservatively dressed Graham. An entertaining contrast. I just hoped Hilary would think so too, and not give slate-man Sid a bad time.

I was poking around trying to find candles for Hilary's beautiful Georgian candlesticks when I saw headlights flash across the windows. Sophie had seen them too, and jumped up to open the door.

"My Lord, what happened to you?" Sophie stood aside so we could all see Sid Colt.

In my mind's eye, I had painted Sophie's new friend as an El Greco type. A sensitive, passive follower of some Eastern philosophic persuasion, wearing, of course, homespun and sandals.

The man we gaped at looked like a burly, unshaven truck driver and was swathed in bandages. He wore sneakers and jeans like every other Vermonter, and a blue work shirt buttoned in two places. It barely covered his bandaged arm held by a sling. The white gauze over his ear and part of his head made his skin look red and feverish.

"Will you let me in looking like this? I won't stay. Just wanted to tell Sophie I was okay, in case she heard about the explosion at the quarry."

We were speechless.

"Guess I should have called," he said.

Hilary was the first to regain his wits. He put his arm around

17

Sid's waist and gently propelled him to the couch and urged him to accept a drink. He'd been bleeding, Sid said, and thought liquor was a poor idea but settled for Hilary's suggestion of tea with a shot of rum. His appearance must have surprised Hilary, too. I could tell from his expression that he was reacting favorably to Sophie's beaten-up new playmate.

"Sorry," Sid said. "I don't know your names."

Sophie responded with apologies and fluttering hands. "My Aunt Letitia McWhinny, your host, Hilary Oats, and Graham Gray. Or is it the other way around?"

"Graham Gray. But my friends call me Gray."

"What's that?" Hilary said, pulling the rum out of the armoire. "Your friends call you gay?"

We had a merry little titter about Hilary's unacknowledged deafness and then zeroed in on Sid's condition.

"Okay, so now tell us, Sid," Sophie said. "What happened?"

"Do you all know what black powder is?" Sid asked.

Gray nodded. I had no idea what black powder was, but nodded too because I didn't want to interrupt his story for a lesson in explosives.

"You know it's gunpowder really, and we use it at the quarry a lot. Unlike dynamite's explosive action, it causes the slate to break up and move, slide, rather than shatter.

"I don't want to bore you. I have to go back," he said. "Sophie knows about the quarry, but I'll tell you . . . "

Sophie came close to shaking Sid. "Come on, come on."

"Well, just this year I inherited the Ethan Allen Slate Company from my uncle who died two years ago. I've been out of the country so they thought maybe I was a goner and planned to sell the outfit to this other company, and the manager Wyman was told he had a berth for life and a free hand in running the place, so you can imagine how he resented me.

"Well, this afternoon he called me over to look at some rock in a new pit and when he went back to his pickup truck, bam-BOOM! I thought I'd bought it.

"Guess I was out of it for a while, and came to propped up between two miners, who delivered me to the Rutland hospital. Another guy drove my car over. They patched me up—sewed up a long cut in my upper arm. They pried some slate out of my ear and taped up a cut on my head. They made me lie down for a couple of hours. And here I am."

"I bet they told you not to drive," Sophie said, "and to go home to bed."

"Right." Sid emptied his teacup and grinned at Hilary. "Really great tea."

I wanted to know if he thought the manager had deliberately tried to hurt him.

"Hurt? Try kill." He drew the side of his hand across his neck. "Dead, out, gone. That's what he wants. But he's out of luck."

"Oh, I don't believe it." Sophie put her hand on his knee. "What are you going to do, Sid?"

"Do? Nothing, really. Just be careful. I figure luck is on my side."

With that brave and cheerful remark, Sid collapsed sideways into Gray's lap. Sophie slid to her knees and took Sid's hand.

"Whew." Sid blinked and winced as he tried to raise his head. "I'm okay. Guess I passed out, but hey, I'm okay."

Well, it wasn't *my* idea of okay, and in seconds I was talking to someone at the Rescue Squad, explaining the situation. She said they might arrive in about twenty minutes.

"I refuse to go back to the hospital." Sid tried to get up without much success. Hilary pinned him with his long index finger and told him to be still and do as he was told.

After Sid was efficiently trundled into the ambulance, we sat down to a subdued dinner.

In spite of our distress, Hilary provided a fine meal. Steak with Sophie's béarnaise sauce, homemade french fries, and stuffed baked tomatoes. We had Sophie's raspberries topped with a dab of soft ice cream.

Gray was an easy conversationalist and we found out more about his life. He blamed his divorce on himself, said that he had worked to the point of exhaustion for years. "Forever," he said. As a partner in an innovative computer company, he had carried a heavy burden, but when the company was bought by a giant rival, "Well," he said, "I took my share of the loot and headed for the hills."

He'd rented the LaPrades' cottage, a small farmhouse far out on one of Lofton's network of dirt roads.

"I've got to learn to breathe all over again," he grinned. "I've even bought a cookbook. That's why I'm interested in your land, Mr. Oats. I want to invest in Vermont, and maybe that could be a beginning." He raised his wine glass. "Who knows?"

When Hilary refused to accept our clean-up services, I think we all parted thinking that Gray was a very nice fellow. An addition to Lofton.

It was clear to me that he went home thinking that Sophie was a star.

THREE

The sun was pouring into my studio, which was beyond the kitchen at the back of the house. I had rigged up shades for the tall windows that pulled from both the bottom and the top, which let me control the light when I painted portraits.

This morning the bright sunshine was unharnessed, and as I bent over my drafting table my back and shoulders almost hummed in the warmth.

The particular thwack that *The New York Times* made when it hit my porch roused Lulu from her post-breakfast nap under the kitchen table.

Delivering my paper was Hilary's idea. I could be a grump the first thing in the morning, so if I didn't respond with a thank-you call he went on home.

"Hilary," I yelled, "wait a minute." I poured us each a mug of coffee and tore open a package of Fig Newtons.

For the thousandth time I blessed my rocking chair. I rocked and munched while Hilary absorbed vital information from the business section.

"So, chum," I said when he'd carefully refolded the paper, "what thoughts do you have on your dramatic little dinner party the other night? How did you like Sid Colt?"

"Bandages always make someone look benign, helpless. Who knows what the man is like?"

"Guess it doesn't really matter what we think since his chance of survival seems slim. Usurping that foreman's position—wow. I wouldn't be in his shoes for a pint of caviar. Good Lord, how would you like to have someone bent on doing you in at a slate quarry? You've seen those places—really frightening."

"As a matter of fact," he said, "I never have. Oh, I've seen those slate dumps sticking up around Fair Haven and Poultney, but I've never actually seen a quarry. But I certainly agree with you, Tish. Don't think I'd want a mortal enemy working with me at a quarry."

He stood up and stretched, touching the ceiling. "Letitia, let's go look at that fella's quarry. I didn't get it quite straight about black powder. Can you make it?"

I could. A portrait I'd been working on was wet as a mud puddle. My model was a vain young girl, her grandmother's darling, who thought she had the flu. Sophie and I would have plenty of other chances to go to Poultney. It was fun exploring with Hil, and I liked the idea of a day off.

That's not to say I worked eight hours a day every day, but more often than not a portrait commission was done on an emergency basis. The subject only had a week to pose, or had to go back to college or back to the Senate, or suddenly lost her two front teeth.

Hilary suggested that we sit on the rim of the quarry and have a picnic lunch. He departed whistling a light-hearted tune, no doubt with visions of creating a new sandwich spread.

Sophie called to say that she was with Sid at the hospital, where the consequences of even a slight concussion had been spelled out in graphic terms. He had to stay another day, and Sophie wanted me to tell Hilary she hadn't forgotten Sid's car was still in his driveway and she'd talk to him later.

Hilary doesn't encourage my participation in gastronomic affairs. Which is all right by me. On one occasion I was stunned when he praised my version of French toast. But how often can you work that into the menu?

First, what clothes to wear to the quarry? I tossed tan corduroy slacks on the bed and added a yellow sleeveless turtleneck to wear under a khaki shirt. The only twinge of envy I had for the young was caused by a ban I'd decreed for myself recently on sleeveless garments, tank tops, and nearly topless bathing suits. I could use a little face-lift along the jawline, too. Oh well, what the hell. Since I wasn't in the performing arts or the CEO of Elizabeth Arden, I figured it didn't matter. I could still do knee bends with the best, stand on my head at the drop of a hat, and wear riding breeches that were made for me more than forty years ago.

Looking in the bathroom mirror, I poked at my short frizzy gray hair, careful not to dislodge my glasses from their usual parking place. My daily make-up consisted of a pat of powder on the end of my nose, a damp finger to urge my eyebrows to go up, and a tame lipstick. I resisted the advice of peers that the seventy-plus group should use brilliant red. It made me feel like a leftover.

Sophie said that in my daytime gear I looked like an old preppie. Oh well, Lulu always looked smart—especially today sporting a black-and-red patent leather collar.

We walked over to the store. I'd heard Mary Cushman, who

used to make lemon squares, was once again delivering those heavenly concoctions of sugar, cholesterol, and magic.

Our village store was a combination of New York's epicurean Dean & DeLuca, a hardware store, a newsstand, and a friendly forum for the collection and dissemination of information.

Beside the embossed, bell-ringing cash register sat a square vintage vitrine. Its four shelves displayed the marvels of local bakers. Wizards like Mary and her lemon squares and old Ralph Spark's towering apple pies. Even Millie, our wonderful librarian, often added her special brownies made with Rice Crispies. A floor-to-ceiling wine rack held thoughtful choices for which Hilary acted as consultant.

T-shirts, cotton kerchiefs, work gloves, and a rack of dark glasses were at the narrow end of the store. To get there you passed diapers, grass seed, soups, crackers, soaps, and a keg of kerosene.

There was just enough of everything—fresh and frozen food and ice cream and penny candy—to keep everyone happy.

The present managers had been hired by a consortium of us who couldn't imagine life without our institution, but were still waiting for an appropriate buyer to appear.

Wanda and Jake Miller were acceptable enough, but some of us felt they lacked a certain vitality and warmth. Jake wasn't so bad, but Wanda was a pretty pouting downer. Efficient and polite, but her accent was on the negative.

Jake, round and pink, peered at me over his rimless glasses to ask which salami I wanted. Hard Genoa, of course. The stuff was my secret vice—a quick fix, a habit I couldn't seem to kick.

The sun hit Jake's balding head as he leaned over the slicer and I felt a moment of compassion that such a plain young man had to accept such an early yardstick of age.

"Six—will that do you, Mrs. McWhinny?" Wanda counted the lemon squares and patted the package of salami. "I wouldn't dare eat anything this fattening."

"Gee, Wanda," I said. The woman was keyhole size. "You've made my day."

I was still fulminating when Hilary appeared, bearing his fitted picnic basket suitable for a group of twelve.

"You don't give a damn about the quarry," I said. "You just wanted an excuse to make lunch."

Fortunately Hilary never rose to the bait when I was in a churlish mood. So I cooled down and gave him the good news that Sid wouldn't be at the quarry. We could snoop on our own.

Fundamentally opposed to guided tours, Hilary had no peer as a snooper and eavesdropper. We had frequently come up with answers to thorny questions because Hilary kept his baby blue eyes and his big ears open.

He put the hamper in the back of my Isuzu Trooper. His ancient Volkswagen Beetle was no longer fit for sorties outside the boundaries of Lofton. It had been wrecked by Father Time, Vermont's winters, and the legions of mice that had dwelt therein.

The chorus of voices urging him to get a new car was swelling. On the brink of conceding, he was still undecided about the Beetle's replacement.

I brought my camera and sketch pad, my cache of lemon squares, and, of course, Lulu.

Sitting on Hilary's lap, she served as an easel for the tourist map Hilary was examining.

"Did you know, so-called Slate Valley runs from Fair Haven and Castleton all the way down to West Pawlet and Rupert? Did you also know that green, gray, and purple slate are found here and that just over the line in New York they have the only

25

red slate quarried anywhere in the world?"

Hilary folded the map. "I don't want you to think my knowledge of slate is confined to a little bit of Vermont geography. Do you think my coffee table books are simply to support your Scotch? I read them."

"I'm listening."

"The largest quarry in Wales, and possibly the world, had a long devastating strike in early eighteen-something which helped to start the industry in the United States. Idle miners poured across the sea in search of work. You can still hear Scottish and Welsh choirs sounding off all up and down Slate Valley."

Hilary interrupted me as I started to sing an old Scottish drinking song. "Please, I'm not finished. Slate was used for tombs as far back as five hundred B.C., and still is. There's a famous slate roof on an eighth-century Saxon chapel on the Avon, and my personal guess is that Cro-Magnon families used slate on their patios—and let's see, Violet le-Duc saved the walled city of Carcassonne from the desecration and rebuilt the place using slate from the nearby Pyrenees. There's a house on Stratton Street built almost entirely of slate from the Ethan Allen Quarry. But it all wouldn't have happened without money."

"Money. I've heard that word before."

"Yes. Well, without railroads connecting the quarries with the rest of the world—fini. So some enterprising New York financiers took care of that." Hilary snapped his fingers. "And they were in business."

"Was Ethan Allen the first quarry?"

"Nope. A quarry in Peach Bottom, Pennsylvania . . . opened in 1734. Now you know everything I know."

I doubted that.

We rolled over the highway from Rutland to Fair Haven,

exclaiming at the sunbathed landscape and the extraordinary variety of yellows and reds.

A mile or so after turning off the highway we came upon an oblong brick building. The sign fixed to a corroded armature on top of the building spelled ETHAN ALLEN SLATE CO. 1887.

A hundred or more flats of cut slate covered a half-acre yard beside the building. We parked and got out, eager to look at the slate which was stacked vertically and divided according to size and color. Poking through the slabs, like prints in a rack, made one want to invent new uses for them. Maybe another bench or a tabletop for Sophie's porch.

Hilary must have felt the same way because he was talking to a man who appeared out of nowhere about buying a piece for his kitchen counter. Would it, he wanted to know, show grease spots?

Apparently puzzled by the question, the man advised us to go to the office.

Hilary raised his eyebrows with the question. I nodded and we were led inside and upstairs and into a rabbit warren of offices.

A busy young woman holding papers in both hands managed to remove the pencil from her mouth and assure Hil that slate didn't show grease spots.

Hilary asked her where to find the quarry.

"It's about two miles over there." She gestured in a northerly direction. "But if you want to visit you'll have to have someone show you around. Today's pretty hectic. Maybe tomorrow?"

We thanked her and left. Aiming north, I asked the first person I saw on the road the way to the quarry. With her instructions, and guided by the increasing number of slate pyramids, we found the Ethan Allen Quarry.

Our first sight was of a collection of dilapidated-looking sheds and huge chunks of uncut slate being carried by mammoth trucks.

In spite of cautionary signs, I drove closer to the buildings and we got our first glimpse of the vast pit.

Hilary got out and I followed, after rolling up the windows to within inches of the top. Lulu obediently stayed in the car and peered through the window, which I usually left open. One look at the depth of the quarry and I wasn't about to take a chance on her usual behavior.

Hilary was standing within a yard of the edge. I held his arm and cautiously peered down at the trucks that looked like match-box toys in the bottom of the pit.

As an acrophobe, even a yard was too close to the edge for me. My problem with heights was a fear of jumping and a fear I'd be undermined by watery knees and collapse into a chasm or out of a window or over a cliff. I couldn't even look at a picture of a person looking over a railing of the Empire State Building without feeling faint.

I think of myself as being normal, whatever that means, but I had another fear that kept me away from the edge.

Snakes. I'd heard that the slate waste piles were the happy home of the Northeast's largest colony of rattlesnakes. Oh, I know they won't bother you if you don't bother them. But it's the very idea of the rattlers that bothers me. Maybe I'm too closely connected to my forebears. Monkeys hate snakes. In any event, I didn't intend to be caught between a rattling viper and the edge of the pit.

"See that sling there?" A sandy-haired workman stopped beside us and lit a cigarette. He pointed to a canvas cradle full of rock being hauled from the bottom up to the surface and dumped into a waiting truck. "That's high. The pit's almost two hundred feet deep, or about the same's a twenty-story build-ing. I don't suppose we have a twenty-story building in all of Vermont."

"How about the rattlesnakes around here?" I asked. "Are they a concern?"

"Naw. You don't see them here where we're working. Was a fella in town who made a living off the rattlesnakes hereabouts. He got a two-dollar bounty for each snake he brought in to the town clerk. She never wanted to look in the bag he had them in and probably paid him for a lot more snakes than was in them. Then he'd go across the line into New York where they paid three dollars for each rattler's tail. Made a good living. Now they're an endangered species. Jesus, can you beat that?"

Finishing his interesting monologue, he looked at his watch and said he hoped we'd have a nice day.

No way, I informed Hilary, would I consider eating lunch on the edge of the roof of a twenty-story building.

Back at the car I put Lulu on a leash and carefully scanned the gray gravel before I let her piddle. Then I hurried back into the safety of my boxy home away from home.

Hilary, with his arms hugging his chest, was talking to a man in khaki pants and a blue polo shirt. Clearly not a laborer, he stood with his hands in his pockets rearranging the gravel with the toe of his boot. I amused myself watching their body lan-guage: confident, poised, yet a little wary.

I was doing a sketch of a small building with an odd-looking apparatus sticking out of its roof when Hilary came back.

"Who's your new friend?"

"Wyman—Edgar Wyman, the manager." Hilary chuckled. "He really seemed surprised when I told him that I knew Sid

29

Colt and all about the accident. The gent doesn't fit my idea of an executioner."

I asked him about black powder.

"The stuff was invented by the Chinese. Our army uses it. Here they drill a hole in the rock and shove in plastic tubing full of black powder. It's easy to get—not chaperoned like dynamite."

"Did he have anything unpleasant to say about Sid? Any cracks?"

"No. But he sounded a little sarcastic when he referred to Colt as numero uno."

"Numero uno. Did he say anything about Sophie?"

"Just that he was interested that I lived not far from her. Said he saw you sketching and said there's going to be an art show of pictures of the quarries. Says he hopes you'll do some drawings around here. You get the dope on it at the Poultney library. We can go by there first and then eat someplace else."

We found out that the library the manager was talking about was not in Poultney but in Granville, New York. The short drive across the border, to what our postmaster Charlie calls York State, was lovely. The landscape was punctuated with ancient slag piles, and trees that had fought their way to daylight from between the slate slabs made a spectacular display, waving their gaudy leaves against the background of black and gray stone. The pyramids looked more like historical monuments than dumps.

Granville, with its solid brick buildings lining the main street, had the distinct flavor of a northern New York State town. We were charmed by the Victorian edifice that housed the library. We parked under a canopy of trees beside a slate retaining wall and walked into a huge reading room, so inviting it could have been my grandfather's living room. I wished we could have lunch there.

A librarian gave me a flyer describing the exhibition and offered the information that her father, a slate miner, had died in a rock slide many years ago. She added, "I give the quarries a wide berth." I didn't blame her. The quarries certainly had pictorial appeal. Not your average postcard variety but a sinister image all its own.

On the way home, we couldn't agree on a picnic site so ended up having a late lunch on my front porch.

My share of the layers of tomatoes, mozzarella, and roasted peppers I put aside for dinner, but I pigged out on Hil's superb sardine sandwiches and, of course, the lemon squares.

FOUR

My aged mare Trixie was a contented boarder at Goat Heaven. I could tell from her greeting that she was as eager as I to take advantage of the glorious fall day. Knowing that Sophie wasn't home, I was surprised to see an unfamiliar car parked on the road a little beyond her house. I didn't pay much attention to the small blue car and let myself into the corral.

A little later in the season and I would have assumed the car belonged to a hunter. Some of them thought they owned the land and parked wherever they chose. However, one well-armed pair might be more cautious another time: Last fall they had parked in the wrong driveway and were met by my friend Hilary and the garden hose.

I should have been a farmer or rancher. Well, no, if I had been I probably wouldn't regard the goats' greeting and Trixie's whinny with such joy.

Trixie displayed her specialty—a wide toothy smile—and delivered what I considered love pats, which involved throwing back her head and banging me with her fuzzy chin.

My lower regions were Rolfed by my special friends in Sophie's goat herd. Along with the usual butting, my chums tried to eat my belt and chewed on vital buttons. This morning a handsome gray nanny I didn't know put her hoof against my stomach and, rising, touched her nose to mine, gazing into my eyes. Given a goat's mysterious oblong optical equipment, that's quite an experience.

The herd took a great interest in the saddling process and Trixie danced around like a colt.

Sophie and I hacked trails through the woods which we also used for cross-country skiing, but I never went on the trails when I rode alone. I could see myself, brushed off by a branch, lying unconscious on the forest floor.

By constant use we had tramped a sort of riding ring around the edge of the corral and out around the far pasture. It wasn't very big, but was just about right for exercising Trixie. There was one stretch where we could canter. The rest of the ring was a rocky slalom course.

Sophie's pride and joy was the barn, a tidy edifice painted red with white trim. Its crowning glory was a jaunty little cupola that had been a Christmas present from Hilary last year.

Even the lovely fall light couldn't help Sophie's house, which slouched on a rock-strewn rise across the road from the barn. I called it a non-house. Many years ago the structure had been assembled by shoving a trailer and a shed together at right angles. A dinky triangular porch held the two parts together.

It wasn't hard to imagine the dark thoughts it must engender at the zoning board and with the members of the garden club, who surely viewed the place as an unfortunate blot on the escutcheon of lovely Clement Hollow.

A noise made me turn in my saddle. Trixie had heard it too

and we stopped to look back at the barn and house.

I don't know how good an old horse's vision is, but mine is very poor and getting worse. My eye doctor said that in another year he'd take my cataracts. I remember thinking it was an odd verb.

The noise we heard must have been the sound of a car door closing, because even without my glasses I could see that the car that had been parked near Sophie's house had started to move up the hill toward Lofton.

I was nearing the barn, patting Trixie's neck and rearranging her mane, when the explosion occurred. The tremendous roar seemed to go right through me. My legs tightened around Trixie and I had a wild image of us both taking off with Dorothy and Toto.

Sophie's house trembled, then rose in the air and, in a split second, crumbled and crashed to the ground.

Trixie, shaking, fell on her knees and in spite of my viselike grip I fell over her head. My fall seemed to be in slow motion and I managed to land on my rump. I rolled over and scrambled to my feet.

Trixie labored to her feet. The goats bleating in terror was a painful sound. Panicked, they were darting about like a school of fish, first in one direction, then another.

All the animals followed me as I rushed with a pounding heart toward the barn.

Timbers and metal sheets were still falling as the dismembered house settled. The chimney fell slowly, sounding like a meandering bowling ball striking the pins. Sophie's cherry-red front door was the only vertical survivor. Hilary's favorite overstuffed armchair had been thrown across the roadway and over the fence, landing upright in the corral. Its curious presence seemed to interest the goats enough to lessen their awful bleating. Clouds of dust spewed out a sour, acrid smell. I thought of it as the ugly building's terminal fart.

I realized the inevitability of fire and could hardly say the word to myself. My vivid imagination had no trouble picturing flames being whipped along by the gusty fall winds and jumping from the kindling on the road, then a few feet more to the barn.

I reasoned the explosion was caused by the gas tanks and I could only think of the pilot light burning under rotten dry wood.

I ran inside the barn to find some pails which I filled at the water trough. The trough, a Victorian bathtub, was fed by a pipe that came from Sophie's house. There was no pressure, no hose, just one drop, pause, then another.

Placing the buckets by the fence, I scurried around and found two more and was filling them when I saw a pickup truck stopped up where the blue car had been parked. The driver jumped out and waved. He cautiously made his way around some of the debris.

"Hey there, anyone hurt?"

I felt weak with relief when I recognized Bob Dirkson, my plumber—everybody's plumber. "Hurry, Bob," I yelled. "Hurry and call for the fire truck!"

Bob barely acknowledged my message, sprinted back to the pickup, and vanished within seconds.

Oh hurry, I said to Trixie, to the goats, to the deities, and especially to the fire fighters. Hurry, Harry, Rex, Murky. I tried to think of the names of more of the men in our volunteer fire department. And Lucy and Mary Beth, new volunteers. Hurry, all of you.

I forced myself to think how many miles it was between Sophie's and the firehouse. How long would it take to round up the fire fighters? Was Mary Beth's beeper beeping right this minute in her beauty parlor? Would they drive by and pick her up? Would she drive here directly?

I remembered where I'd seen more pails and ran down to the old pig sty under the barn and came back with two more.

Before I saw it I smelled the smoke. Gray puffs appeared above where the kitchen had been.

Oh God, the wind. I closed my eyes and put my forehead against Trixie's neck. Come on, hurry—repeating my litany of names.

"Jesus Q. Christ, what happened, lady? Did the gas blow?"

Trixie was glad to get out of my clutches as I turned to the man whose T-shirt said PAY DIRT and saw that he had driven up from the other direction in a five-ton gravel truck.

"Anyone in there?"

Not for an instant had it crossed my mind that a person or a creature could be in the house. I knew Sophie was playing in a tennis tournament. There were no pets in the house since Sophie's brother had gone off to college with his bat Brownee who lived in an umbrella.

That was the first moment that I gave any thought to the car I'd seen. Had someone been dropped off? I shuddered.

"You okay? Hey, here comes the fire engine."

Fire engine. What beautiful words. They sounded like the first chord of a love song—or the opening of a lyric poem. Fire engine.

I backed up to the mounting block and suppressed a howl as I sat heavily on my sore bottom.

Seventy-three was too old for all this, I thought. I should be playing bridge or having my nails done or be reading Horace, Proust, or Sue Grafton. Not sitting with my wet feet in manure with my clothing being nibbled by goats.

"I'm sorry, dear." I apologized to Madonna, a particularly insistent nanny who was trying to remove my caper-sized left earring. Her effort involved snorting in my ear and I'd hit her quite hard.

Rising with difficulty, I made my way along the fence to greet the fire fighters. They waved and went about their business of strapping canisters on each other's backs. Then holding the yard-long nozzles ahead of them, they rushed up and out of sight behind the smoking jackstraw pile of timbers that had been the kitchen.

The water hissing on the timbers sounded like oil bouncing on a hot pan. The smoke turned into a mushroom cloud, then scattered and began to fade.

Lucy saw me as she ran down the hill. "Hiya, Tish. Gotta call the troopers."

Lucy was my accountant. Her office was in the front of her house in Londonderry. Visits with her were advisable during school hours as she was the mother of six children.

When she returned she demanded a blow-by-blow description of what she called "The Event." She, too, wanted to know if anyone had been in the house.

The truck driver allowed as how if that was the case whoever it was would be dead as a doornail.

One of the fire fighters, Murky Waters, who was also our road commissioner, said he was going to try to get hold of Turk Smith who was working on the tractor over on Shorts' Hill to see if he could come over and move some of the debris off the road.

"Lucy, bring that cop up to the scene just as soon as he comes, okay?"

We'd gathered quite a crowd by then, with cars blocked on either end of the mess. Most of them were friends or acquaintances, and I repeated what little I knew over and over.

Soon we welcomed Turk Smith's noisy arrival. He was not my favorite person. He turned off his machine and came over to consult with Murky. We exchanged a minimal greeting.

Turk pushed his cap back on his head, gave his scalp a good scratch. "Jesus, Murky, what the fuck happened? Gas tanks?"

Murky nodded. He held up his hand as Turk started toward the house. "Not now. Gotta wait for the cops."

"Cops?"

"Yeah. An explosion is not a natural happening. So let's put you to work."

They moved out of hearing.

"Pew," Lucy said, holding her nostrils. "How can anyone smell that bad?"

"You mean Turk?" We both smiled. It seemed a shallow reason for not liking someone. It was more than his smell. It was those mean shoe-button eyes and his innate rudeness. Last year Turk had started a business of collecting people's garbage. I subscribed, and one day I came home to find him in my kitchen, which gave me an uneasy feeling, so I terminated his services, explaining that I really liked to go to the dump. I'm happy to say he wasn't a product of Lofton. He was a leftover from one of the construction crews that blanketed our area in the eighties.

I had been dreading what happened next.

First I heard her rattletrap station wagon, then I could hear her yelling as she ran between the line of cars and gawkers toward the house.

Sophie, in white shorts, a sweatshirt, and tennis sneakers, ran over to the corral fence and wrapped her arms around the top rail and sagged. Her breathing was the only sound. Murky spoke to the people milling about. "Why don't you all go on your way. Turk's made some room there, you can all get by. Come on, now. Let's move it."

A friend of Sophie's came forward to her with an outstretched hand, but thought better of it and retreated.

Sophie had the icy look of someone in shock. She pulled herself up and turned to me. "Who did it, Tish?"

"Who did it?" I smiled wanly. "Guess it was the gas tanks— they exploded."

Shaking her head, she wandered over to the armchair, and pushing goats away, collapsed in the butt-sprung survivor. "Tish . . ." I followed and stood beside the chair. "Tish, the gas tanks were *empty.*"

FIVE

My tired reactors made an effort to process what Sophie had told me, which accounted, I guess, for my dazed expression when I turned to see who was speaking to me.

"It's Mrs. McWhinny, isn't it? Are you okay?"

The young uniformed state trooper took my arm and led me back to the mounting block, where we both sat down.

"The fire chief tells me that you witnessed the explosion."

"Yes I did, officer, and there isn't much to tell." But I described the picture fixed in my mind. The only part of my account that seemed to interest him was the unidentified car.

"What color blue, ma'am?"

"Pale blue."

"Powder blue?"

"I don't know what powder blue is. It's cerulean blue—a smidgen of black and a lot of white."

As I described the color with such certainty, I remembered that my eye doctor had said a sign of cataracts was a misperception of blues.

"I see," he said. "Two doors or four doors?"

I didn't know. We discussed makes of cars and I had to confess I could only recognize kinds that were distinctive. Rolls Royces, Volvo wagons, and assorted vintage cars. All small shiny new cars looked alike to me. And as for the license plates and bumper stickers he asked me about, I just couldn't remember.

"I have to ask you to wait here a little longer, Mrs. McWhinny. Someone from Montpelier wants to talk to you. Luckily she was nearby. Maybe twenty minutes."

I nodded and followed him over to where Sophie was still sitting in the chair. She held a brown-and-white kid in her arms.

"I've lost everything," she wailed to the officer. "I haven't even got a pair of blue jeans. I've lost my camera, my books, pictures, and my earrings. Oh God, my earrings."

"Hey, I know it seems awful." The officer patted her shoulder. "But there was hardly any fire. Nothing's burned. Only breakable things are broken." He smiled. "It'll be okay."

Then he asked Sophie to wait for a government agent to arrive.

"What government? What agent?"

"An agent from the Treasury Department of Alcohol, Tobacco and Firearms."

That brought Sophie to her feet. "So what's this all about? "

"Not my job, lady. You'll find out soon enough. And hey— good luck."

Sophie and I both seemed to sense the futility of a guessing game and began to pace to and fro among the goats.

Murky and the state trooper stood by the corral gates and we heard Sophie's neighbors being told they couldn't talk to us now.

"Can't talk to us! This is spooky as hell, Tish. I feel like a criminal."

41

"Yeah, like a couple of jailbirds."

In about ten minutes a white coupe stopped behind the fire truck and a smartly dressed young woman emerged. She looked around and beckoned to the state trooper. We watched them shake hands and, with the fire fighters, walk up behind the house.

Sophie tore through the gate and ran after them.

I wasn't about to run anyplace. The thought of putting my bruised fanny on the mounting block one more time was unbearable, so I walked to where my car was parked and slid slowly into the driver's seat. Resting my head on the steering wheel I massaged the back of my neck.

My semiconscious state was altered by Sophie's voice. "Tish, this is Sue Rawby."

"Mrs. McWhinny, hello. I'm from the Treasury Department. I want to tell you what I told your niece."

I looked into steady brown eyes in an oval, pleasantly designed face.

"The explosion was caused by dynamite." She waited a moment, watching the shocking news age my face. "Our policy is to keep any incident involving dynamite out of the news. Papers, television. And to avoid such episodes from becoming common knowledge."

"Why?" I asked.

"The illegal use of dynamite is a very serious offense, and any leaks about what happened here today will hamper our investigation. I'm sure I can rely on your discretion."

Still stunned, I assured her she could. I silently admired her well-manicured nails when she handed me her card.

"If you have any thoughts about the explosion or any recollections about the small car you saw, it's vital that you call me."

Sophie walked with Agent Rawby back to her car and watched

her leave. She shook hands with the volunteers and hugged Lucy. After she waved goodbye to the trooper, she once again sagged against the fence and gazed at the pathetic jumble of planks and pots and shattered glass that once was her house.

"Come on, dear," I called, opening the passenger's door. "Get in."

She climbed in and slammed the door. Her sorrow was turning to rage.

"What rotten, stinkin', fuckin' creep would bomb my house? My house! Who hates me?"

"No one hates you, Sophie. Don't think that for a moment. There must be some other explanation."

"And you, I suppose," Sophie said bitterly, "are going to find out what it is."

"It's possible, but improbable. Now, in spite of your sarcasm, dear girl, I'm taking you to the Clothes Mart. Don't argue. It's on me."

On the short drive to Londonderry, Sophie, silent, kept her head turned away, but I could see her grim expression reflected in the window.

My own dark thoughts were lightened by the thought of Agent Rawby. She looked so competent and I felt sure she had many professional helpers and unlimited technical aids. I hoped that by tomorrow some unrelated kook would be in handcuffs and the whole grisly mess would be solved.

Marie Miller, who was in charge of women's clothing at the Mart, was a model of tact and efficiency.

I told her briefly about the explosion and she led Sophie away. I could see them yanking slacks and shirts off the hangers and piling their arms full of sweaters and Lord knows what all.

Since I knew Sophie's shoe size, I ducked over to the shoe

outlet and bought fuzzy slippers, soft canvas boots, and a fistful of socks. We made another brief stop at the drugstore before heading home.

We both saw Turk Smith's truck parked in front of the pub.

"He didn't waste any time," I said. "Wonder what he's celebrating."

"Maybe," Sophie said, "it's because he doesn't own the house anymore."

"Turk owned your house?"

"Yeah. He lost it to the bank quite a while ago. Remember? I bought it from them."

Hilary was in Boston, and even though I missed him when he was away, I was relieved not to have to describe the explosion one more time. Hilary thought fine food could cure most ills, so I was grateful to be spared the effort of holding myself together and being properly appreciative of his efforts. The only thing I wanted to do was soak my rear end in a hot tub and reflect on the day's profoundly puzzling event.

Sophie made two trips to take her new wardrobe upstairs to the yellow guest room. In moments I heard my antique spindle bed groan under her weight.

I followed her example and a couple of hours later, feeling limp and not at all refreshed, I came downstairs with tea in mind. I found Sophie wearing skinny new jeans, a white shirt, and the fuzzy slippers. She had taken over the library telephone.

I gathered she was talking to the insurance company. I remembered they had insured the barn for a reasonable amount and allocated a tiny sum for the dilapidated house.

Sophie joined me in the kitchen and said they wanted her to give them twenty-four hours to inspect the place before she tackled the cleanup.

"Can you collect from them even though the house was blown up? Isn't there something about natural causes?"

"She said she didn't know. I hesitated to tell them about it. I'll ask Sue Rawby. Lord, I didn't know the government made such a big deal about dynamite. She told me you have to apply to her agency to even buy the stuff. Even after you get it they monitor the supply every month to see that you're doing whatever you said you were going to do with it. She also said anyone smelling the explosion would know it was dynamite. She said that the fire chief knew the smell and called their 800 number."

"Thank goodness they weren't trying to do away with you."

"What makes you think they weren't?"

"If the dynamiter wanted to harm you it would have been rigged differently. You know, been set to go off if you turned on a light switch or something like that. He knew you weren't home. Maybe the garden club did it."

Sophie looked offended at my attempt at humor.

Lulu's barking heralded a caller and I opened the front door for Graham Gray.

"I just heard about your house." He looked rosier and younger in the daylight. "I drove by to see if there was anything I could do. Sophie, let me help you. My mother said I could clean up a mess better than anyone else. And I'm a finder. I find lost things."

Sophie's tired young face softened. She was clearly touched by Gray's persuasive offer of help.

I made tea for all of us. At the last minute I changed my libation to Scotch.

Gray said that some people he talked to said it was caused by a car bomb.

Sophie shrugged. "I bet there'll be dozens of stories. The police want us to be quiet about the whole thing. You know, until

45

they find out whether it was the gas tanks or whatever."

Moving into the library, I shuffled papers on my desk, only half listening to them talk.

I heard Sophie ask, "But who in the world would have access to dynamite?"

I knew and so did Gray. "How about your friend who owns the slate quarry?" he asked.

"That's crazy. I mean we, you know, like each other. He wouldn't blow up my house. And what would be the point?"

Gray asked Sophie if she knew anyone in a construction crew—or road builders or excavators. "Or anyone else at the quarry. Maybe one of the guys is jealous of Sid. Like me"—he smiled—"I'm jealous of him."

Sophie laughed. "So someone's jealous. They nuke my house so I'll fall into their arms? Crazy."

No longer listening, I watched a bizarre and lovely rite of fall practiced by my neighbor Kitty.

Kitty, a cheerful octogenarian, leaned on the handle of her spade as she looked down at the hole she had just dug at the end of her flowerbed.

I watched her pick up a large oval-shaped pumpkin—and, placing it carefully in the hole, cover it with earth, patting down the top layer with obvious satisfaction.

Ten years ago when I first observed this procedure I rushed outside to question her sanity.

It was her grandmother's recipe, she said. Remove the seeds from a Vermont pumpkin, fill the cavity with brown sugar, and bury it till spring—creating a wicked and delicious liquor.

When I emerged from the library, Sophie and Gray had gone. A note taped to the newel post said: OFF TO FEED THE GOATS. DON'T WAIT UP.

Six

The telephone rang at eight in the morning. It was Agent Sue Rawby. She wanted to speak to Sophie.

Sophie, clad in nothing but a long black T-shirt and the fuzzy slippers, took the telephone and said, "Yes, sure. Of course. Okay." She hung up. "Hope you don't mind, Tish. She's coming over soon. She's in Weston."

It was a good excuse to use the cornbread mix I'd had in a cabinet for years. A friend once advised me to add another egg to any box of mix, so I thought, what the hell, if she thought one extra egg helped, I'd add two.

Jeans and a turtleneck sweater made Sue ("Call me Sue"— "Call me Tish") look less official. She might have been a friend of Sophie's instead of her inquisitor.

"This is marvelous." Sue was trying to butter a wedge of cornbread the consistency of a soufflé. "I love spoon bread. What a beautiful room. Aside from a view of the Capitol's gold dome, I live in a dark, dreary apartment building."

My antique Kashmir rug always did look beautiful in the

sunlight. I was partial, too, to the burnt-orange fabric on my sofa and the melon-colored draperies that wrapped the room in warmth. Hilary called my walls eggnog white, a perfect background for a dozen paintings and the long gold mirror over the mantel. "Let me know," Sue said, putting Lulu in her lap, "if you ever need a house and dog sitter."

"Is there any news about the explosion? Anything new?"

"Yes, we know the source of the dynamite. Dynamite is impregnated with small chips of colored plastic called tagnets that in an explosion become a gluelike consistency and adhere to matter at the site. The identifying chips were instantly visible to me at your house, Sophie, and once back at the office it was only a matter of minutes to find the application and shipping orders. The dynamite was from the lot sent to the Ethan Allen Slate Company in Poultney. Are you acquainted with anyone there?"

Sophie was speechless, so I rushed in and said we both knew the owner of the company.

"I've only met him once. My niece knows him better." I excused myself and went into the kitchen and only half heard Sophie describing her brief relationship with Sid Colt. If Sue Rawby was pressing her for intimate details, I didn't want to hear them.

"Tish," Sophie called, "come back."

Sue wanted to know if I had any connection to the quarry or knew anyone else there. So I described Hilary's and my visit and told her I had planned to go back and do drawings around the quarry.

"Tomorrow, perhaps. Not today. We have a full team working over at the quarry. They're questioning the workers and exploring all possibilities."

Shortly after Sue left, someone from the insurance company came to tell Sophie she could begin clearing. After a siege on the phone, Sophie arranged for a truck and two men to meet her at the farm at noon.

First, she said, she was going to the clinic. Gray had persuaded her that she should have a tetanus shot before tossing around jagged sheets of metal and boards with rusty nails.

I wondered if the sensible young man was going to edge out Sid in Sophie's fickle affections.

When she took off to feed the goats I settled down in my serene little kitchen where Lulu and I finished the rest of the cornbread.

By five o'clock the house was bedlam. Hilary arrived with bags of goodies from Boston and had to be filled in on the bombing and the finger-pointing at Ethan Allen.

Hilary took up so much room and always had so many things—food, pots, bags, papers, and his messy pipe. He could create bedlam all by himself. Having been away, he thought his cat, Vanessa, was lonely, and had brought her along. She wasted no time making herself at home. Within minutes I saw her on the kitchen counter nibbling the chunk of gorgonzola I'd put out for hors d'oeuvres.

Sid must have come in very quietly because, unwittingly, I walked in on Sid and Sophie embracing in the library. It wasn't a very sexy hug. Sophie seemed to be hanging on to Sid for support.

He left Sophie to droop by herself and came over to me. "My hand works today." His bandages had shrunk to major Band-Aids. "Sophie invited me for dinner. Are you sure it's not too much trouble?"

Sid, like Sophie, had thick dark eyebrows that almost met in

49

the middle. But on Sophie they looked better. Hers were carefully groomed and tilted up at the ends, giving her patrician face an unexpected pixie look.

I'd have to get within inches to form an opinion of Sid's malamute eyes, which didn't seem appropriate at the moment.

He was built like a piece of pie—massive shoulders, a tiny waist, zero hips, and small feet. The pie-slice image was accented by his open collar revealing a V of black hair.

Hilary would have a fit. I'd never heard him complain about bare-shouldered women in evening dresses at a dinner party, but he frowned on men who exhibited any anatomy below the Adam's apple.

Sid was dressed much as Sophie had originally described him. He was wearing a tangerine homespun shirt that looked great in my living room, baggy, burlap pants tight at the ankle, and expensive-looking sandals.

Even critical Hilary would have to admit the man had nice manners.

Over drinks and what was left of the gorgonzola, Sid described what had gone on at the quarry.

A team of six Treasury agents had appeared at the Ethan Allen office and spent all morning questioning the employees and poring over records.

The team spent the afternoon at the quarry, doing the same thing.

"While they were investigating Sophie's disaster, did these investigators go into your brush with fate?" I asked. "Or doesn't black powder rate their attention?"

"Naw. That was strictly an accident, quote-unquote, could happen to anybody, says Wyman."

"They're coming back again tomorrow. They want to talk to

every worker, all seventy of them. We were supposed to ship out some orders today. Forget about it. Everything came to a stop."

"Who could have done it, Sid?" Sophie asked. "I mean, can anyone, like, take a stick of dynamite and just walk off with it?"

"No, the building that holds the dynamite has one door and an unbreakable lock. The detonators are in another block building, locked. There are only four keys. I have one. Had to give it to one of the guys there today. The manager has one and the pit foreman has one. And one other is kept in the office. And nobody knows from nothing. Nobody sits and watches the office key. It's on a hook by my desk. But no one wants to fool with dynamite if they don't have to. Wyman, the manager, says he didn't have anything to do with it. The foreman, an old guy who was practically born in the quarry, says he didn't. "

"When there's no apparent motive," I said, "how do you find out who's guilty? An age-old question."

"I can promise you, Mrs. McWhinny, I'm going to find out. We can't have some kook after Sophie." He reached over and squeezed Sophie's hand. "I'll find him."

Sid seemed in charge of the direction of the conversation and soon was asking Hilary about his land. He surprised us all.

"I fell in love with Lofton about eight years ago. I hiked all over the mountain and behind your house, on your land. Didn't know it was yours at the time. I was up here for a couple of weeks with a movie crew. I was general handyman and gofer. Remember *Baby Boom?*"

Of course we did. It had been a lively time for Lofton and involved all of us who lived in the middle of town.

"Sid knows Wanda and Jake, you know," Sophie said.

"No, I didn't know. Did you tell them about Lofton?" I asked. "Or the other way around?"

"No. Hadn't seen either of them since school. Barely knew Jake. I was as surprised when I walked in the store as they were."

Hilary wanted to know why he hadn't stayed after the movie, in view of the fact that his uncle had a slate quarry in Vermont.

"My father and my uncle weren't close. In fact, they didn't like each other at all and I grew up in a mining town. Scranton. We lived in a house that sagged. I always thought it was going to fall into the mine under us. So the idea of a quarry was, if you'll excuse the expression, the pits. Never crossed my mind to even go see the place. I certainly never thought I'd inherit it."

"That land of yours, Mr. Oats, it's so beautiful, overlooking Lofton. What a view."

"Well, young man, I'll tell you. A couple of years ago when I rewrote my will, I left the entire acreage to one person, and since then it's been an old man's amusement to entertain offers and hear what various people had in mind for the property.

"Actually, it's never been on the market, and now's the time, I think, to put a halt to speculation about it. It's not fair."

"One person, Hil," I said. "I thought you were the solo, one-and-only, incomparable Oats in existence."

"Right. But who says it has to go to an Oats? What's wrong with a Beaumont?"

Sophie squealed and flung her arms out. I saw the blood spurt as she hit Sid on the nose. Then she jumped up and wound her long arms around Hilary.

We left them babbling as I led Sid to the bathroom and gave him a washcloth.

When she calmed down, Sophie made Sid lie on the couch with his head in her lap while she pressed ice cubes on either side of his nose.

"If I can't have that land, Mr. Oats, I'm sure glad Sophie can.

But you can't get rid of me that easily. I really love this place."

When we were alone, Hilary discussed his stunning gift of land to Sophie.

"I told her there were strings attached, but not in writing. For instance, I think she should give the top section to the National Forest. Also told her I'd give her some financial help to build something small, a place to live at the farm. Then by the time I cork off—tomorrow or ten years from now—she'll have a better idea of what direction her life is taking and what to do. And hell, Tish, who better to leave it to?"

"You're a generous old coot, Hil, and Sophie's a very lucky young woman."

"It gives me pleasure to think of Sophie in charge. She's an environmental baby and I know she'll do the right thing."

"You should tell Gray yourself, Hil. He was a serious bidder and he'll be disappointed."

"I will. Sid didn't seem upset. But then maybe I wouldn't know if he were."

"Have you considered," I said, "that Sophie's future is subject to change? For example, I've heard a lot of talk from her about babies lately."

"Oh, that's ridiculous. She's too young."

"Young! She's twenty-seven. Granted, she may not be worried about her biological clock yet, but she's definitely in a nesting mood."

"Are you suggesting, Tish, that she may marry this Sid Colt?"

Shielding a yawn, I assured Hilary that I had no inside information and that I was silly to have brought up the subject. Even if she wanted to marry a flagpole sitter, I told him, we'd have no say in the matter.

SEVEN

Lying in bed the next morning, I thought about the quarry, concentrating on the four keys to the blockhouse where the dynamite was kept.

Common sense made me rule out the foreman as a suspect. He'd probably never heard of Sophie, nor had even been to Clement Hollow. And the old pit boss possibly hadn't been farther south than Rutland in years.

They could, I reasoned, have opened the shed and handed a box or a couple of sticks of dynamite to anyone, unaware of the recipient's intentions.

The blockhouse key on a hook in Sid's office was available to anyone, too. Who wanted it? No one could think Sid would blow up his true love's house. As Sophie said, it's crazy. And Sid didn't strike me as crazy.

Edgar Wyman, the bitter manager, seemed the most likely suspect. Was he trying to discredit Sid as the new quarry owner? Since everyone at the quarry probably knew the dynamite would be identified, why bring such unfortunate attention to Ethan

Allen? What was in it for Wyman? Or maybe he was crazy. My mind wasn't functioning. I decided to rely on my eyes. Maybe they'd tell me something. Maybe help trigger the thinking process.

No one paid any attention to me as I drove through the quarry gate and proceeded at three miles an hour to the west rim of the pit.

With Lulu safely in the car, I prowled around with my camera. Each step I took was with a timber rattler in mind. The only rattle came from far below, where the jackhammers were stuttering on the slate. A different sound was the thumping of the pump that kept the water at the bottom of the pit under control.

Even though the water reflected the bright blue sky above, something about it seemed ominous. I wondered what was hidden under that glassy surface. Probably nothing more sinister than junked cars and trucks.

Through my camera lens I saw the dynamite hut for the first time. Gingerly, I got back into the car and drove around the pit, trying to shrink as I passed bulldozers and gargantuan trucks piled high with slabs of slate of Stonehenge proportions.

Out of the car again, I assumed a firm stance and aimed my camera at the cinder-block building.

Before I could press the release, a hand the size of a fielder's mitt grabbed my arm. With his other huge hand, the man seized my camera and yanked its strap over my head, knocking off my glasses. "Gimme that." I felt wet lips on my ear. "You're out of bounds." His voice was as brutal as his hands.

Hilary had suggested that in some previous incarnation I must have been an acrobat. Or possibly my agility was due to devotion to yoga. I tried to kick the man in the crotch. However, age and a lack of practice brought the toe of my boot in stunning contact with his shin instead of my target. It sounded like a pistol shot.

Yelling obscenities, the hulk tried to pull me toward the edge of the quarry. Twisting like a ferret, I bit his wrist.

As the man howled in pain, he was surrounded and restrained by a posse of men. One of them picked up my glasses and handed them to me. Unbroken, thank goodness. Dreading it, I put my index finger in my mouth to see if my new bridge was still there and reassure myself that I hadn't left the expensive trio of teeth in the man's wrist. The tooth fairy must have been watching over me. No gaping holes.

Weak with pain, I leaned against a manly chest, and recognized the manager. He was patting my shoulder.

"Oh, Mr. Wyman—you are my savior. I thought that man was going to kill me." The others were leading my assailant away. "Who is the brute?"

"You just bit a Treasury agent, ma'am. But I didn't see any blood, so I guess it will be all right. Did you know a human's bite is . . ."

"I know. More dangerous than a dog's. I think he broke my arm. Is there a doctor around? Or a clinic?"

Wyman gently guided me around to the passenger side of my car and helped me in. He got in the driver's seat.

Lulu took exception to a stranger behind the wheel. She seated herself firmly in my lap and produced her version of a growl. Neither of us spoke as we drove along the winding road to town. Pain took precedence over manners, but our silence did give me a chance to take a good look at Edgar Wyman.

His face had been modeled with clumsy fingers. The effect was bumpy but not unpleasant. His Airedale hair and broad, flat mustache gave him a kind of style. His voice I knew could be heard over the quarry clatter.

"That was a dangerous thing to do, ma'am, biting someone. You could catch something, you know."

"Something? Oh Lord, you mean like AIDS?"

"Yup. I'm not saying that the agent has AIDS. But biting is a bad idea."

Chastened, I shivered in silence until we reached the clinic.

Once there, I felt pretty woozy waiting for the doctor, and worse when he prodded my swelling arm. After examining the X ray, he pronounced my arm injured. I knew that. But not broken. The young doctor told me to expect profound coloration. I was then dismissed.

There was a point in the next few minutes when kind Edgar Wyman must have wished the cretin had pushed me into the pit. He was insistent on taking me home. I refused. It took a lot of histrionics and a mini–conniption fit to persuade him that I was quite capable of driving.

He turned down my offer to drive him back to the quarry and said he'd walk to his house, which was nearby.

As I drove toward Lofton, the pain in my arm was lessened by the gratitude I felt for being alive.

My plans for the evening were to continue to do what I had been doing all afternoon at home—pamper myself. Lie on the couch, read, snooze. Watch my arm turn blue.

But it was not to be. Just when I was trying to decide whether I had the energy to get up and pour myself a drink, Sophie appeared. She held the door open for Sid, who came in carrying a box, and what I at first took to be a roll of canvas, but which turned out to be a picture screen. I thought the box must be full of slides. My heart sank.

It wasn't dark yet, so no doubt Sophie had invited Sid for dinner. I wanted to scream, but instead rose to my full height of five-foot-three and marched over to the mahogany washstand that served as my bar, intending to pour myself a drink. For the second time that day, something was taken out of my hand. Hilary, who had come in unannounced, took the bottle away from me, kissed the top of my head, and poured us drinks. "Caught you, Letitia. You wouldn't want to drink alone."

The notion that there should be guilt attached to drinking alone puzzled me. If a body wants a drink, what earthly difference does it make if one's alone, with a friend, or among millions?

Lulu welcomed another arrival. Graham Gray. He presented me with a perfect melon squash. I heard myself inviting him for dinner, too.

All at once the assembled group realized my arm was in a sling. That the sling was my finest scarf may have made them think old Aunt Tish was just trying to be a little different.

I was escorted to the wing chair, cooed over, and handed things I didn't need. Sid even brought me a footstool.

I recounted the morning's events to a rapt audience.

Sid leaned over me. "Does it hurt?"

"Like hell. Your manager Wyman gets an A-plus. I'd probably be at the bottom of Lake Ethan Allen if he hadn't come along."

Hilary wanted to know about the Treasury agent. "Is he going to sue you?"

"I hope not. I left word at Sue Rawby's office that I was sorry—sort of."

The exciting news of the evening was that Hilary had bought a new car. Sophie, followed by her two admirers, went outside to look at it. I declined and told Hil a verbal description would be sufficient.

"An old man's car," he said. "Forty thousand miles on it, a dirty gray, and quite inexpensive. The expensive part was getting them to move the seat back three feet so I could get in the thing."

For dinner Hilary created a great pasta dish of fusilli, sausage, and snow peas with a yogurt and blue-cheese sauce. Sophie made an heroic salad, and over coffee we took our places for the slide show.

Even an amateur photographer can't louse up the gorgeous Himalayas and toothy Sherpas poking lumbering yaks.

"That's you?" Sophie made Sid pause while we focused on a man with a full black beard wearing the orange garb of the holy.

"Yup, that's me. You like a beard? I can grow one like that"— he snapped his fingers—"in a week."

"Who took these pictures of you?" Gray asked. "Were you part of a group?"

"Naw. I'd pick up a friend, a fellow traveler along the way. The hospitality was something else. We never had to buy a meal."

Sophie laughed. "You mean never ever in two years—or was it three?"

"Two. Oh, we helped out. I watched some guy's goat herd for him." He stuck a finger in Sophie's side. "What did I tell you? Goats love me. And we worked on an old man's house."

"But the orange that you're wearing. Isn't that for Hare Krishna or religious people?"

"Yes and no. It doesn't matter. No one knows whether you're really holy or not. So I let 'em think I was."

"Are you a yogi?" I asked.

Sid rose, put his hands in prayer position and nodded his head. "Om shanti."

It was too painful for me to respond in kind but I did like the serene and gracious greeting.

"Sophie has told me that you're enthusiastic about yoga."

Enthusiastic didn't sound like a yogic word to me. I confessed that I didn't embrace yoga philosophy, simply from a lack of interest, but I loved Hatha Yoga—the practice that limbers and stretches one's body.

Sid's callous attitude contrasted dramatically with the high-minded and devoted yogis I had known. The idea that anyone would pretend to be a holy person, for whatever reason, struck me as offensive. But I was in no mood for a philosophic discussion. In fact, my only interest was in going to bed.

"It must be hard," Hilary said, "after that life, to work in an office. In fact, be responsible for the whole place?"

"You better believe it. It's only the thought of living around here that keeps me at it."

"I would think the quarry would be a fascinating challenge for you," Hilary said.

"What's a challenge is how I'm going to live the rest of my life." He smiled at Sophie. "The slate business is so labor-intensive, there's no making a fortune there."

"A fortune? What's the matter," Hilary asked, "with making a living?"

"Oh, sure—it will keep me busy for a while."

I was relieved that Sid didn't seem to want to go on and discuss his future. Gray had been rather quiet all evening, and that suited me just fine. I wished they'd all be overcome by a vast yawn and say goodnight.

"I have some slides, too, Mrs. McWhinny." Gray was the

first to rise. "But you'll be glad to know I didn't bring them tonight."

"Oh, wonderful," I said.

"Tish means," Sophie said, "we'd love to see them some other time."

"If you were roaming around India, how did you hear about your uncle's death?"

I could have crowned Hilary. He seemed bent on quizzing Sid, while I sat with my head in my hands, literally holding my eyelids up.

"A letter. My landlady sent me a letter in New Delhi. We'd agreed she'd send me anything that seemed really important to me at American Express in both New Delhi and Nepal. I hit both places a couple of times and a letter from her four or five months ago told me about inheriting the quarry and that everyone was trying to find me.

"That very same day in Delhi I talked to a man who knew all about slate. An Indian. He had even imported slate to America."

"With all the slate here?" Gray said. "Why do we need Indian slate? Is it some special color?"

"Hey. This is an international business. The industry needs a global market. India's slate is low grade but suitable for certain uses. This guy told me about an agent that dealt in slate as real estate, you know, quarries. Said he was smarter than a fox, said I should go see him. One little problem, his headquarters were in Suriname."

"Where?" Sophie asked.

"It used to be called Dutch Guiana. So, we went."

"One moment, Sid," Hilary said. "Your travels in India don't sound exactly deluxe. How did you get to Suriname?" He rubbed his thumb and index finger together. "I mean money."

Sid laughed. "That's when Wyman fell in love with me for the first time. When I called and asked for five grand. And that's not all. When we got there, this agent had moved to Nassau. But we had a great time in Suriname anyway. You can make a mint there if you're fast on your feet. There was this one guy . . . " Sid leaned back and crossed his legs in what the politicians might call a story-telling mode. I was no longer sleepy. "I didn't know this guy. But by snitching just one little form from the export office he parlayed a deal buying and selling sugar that made him a cool three mil."

"That," Gray said, "was quite a brainstorm."

"But not exactly honorable, right?" That comment was from Hilary, who I could see had been offended by Sid's gleeful recitation of the guy's perfidy.

"Not exactly, but very clever. But anyhow, we went on to Nassau."

"We?" I asked.

"My friend and I. This Indian agent was really super. We spent a whole day talking about slate and the world market. He had all kinds of ideas."

"Ideas?" Hilary looked as chilly as Mount Rushmore.

"About business." Sid smiled and shook his head. "I mean the guy sizzles."

Thank goodness Hilary said goodnight, followed by Gray, who helped Sid out with his slides.

Sophie insisted on doing the dishes, and said she'd walk Lulu and bring her up to bed later.

As an old loner, I didn't know if I could take these gatherings every night. I wasn't sure I could pull through until Sophie cleaned up her site and built a house. Even the most basic house probably couldn't be built before first snowfall. I vowed to talk to Sybil York, a realtor friend, about apartments for Sophie. I wanted to be sure there was something available before I tried to reclaim my semi-solitude.

When Sophie tiptoed in with Lulu I was still wide awake, and patted the side of the bed.

"Tell me, dear, how did you meet Sid, and what do you know about him?"

"You don't like him."

I denied any such feelings.

Sophie said she had met Sid through Wanda and Jake Miller, which I knew. They had all lived in Scranton. "I admit, Tish, his profile's a little hard to figure, but he's so imaginative and he's fun."

She didn't need to tell me that he was sexually attractive. That message came through loud and clear. Maybe it was the combination of his animal vitality and those eyes. His pale eyes shaded by black brows and long dark eyelashes probably sent the same message to most women he met. As in "Hey, lady, lie down, I want to talk to you."

"How about Gray? He certainly has worked his heart out for you. He must really be jealous of Sid."

"Jealous? Nothing like that. I guess he was disappointed when I told him about the land, but he said there were lots of other beautiful places in Vermont and he was going to stick around and find one. Sid likes Gray. Thinks he's smart. As a matter of fact, he said he's like to persuade him to work at the quarry."

"I'm surprised at that. It seemed to me that their relationship, brief as it was, was sort of guarded."

"Guarded. There you go, reading things into things that don't add up. Relax." Changing the subject, she went on. "Tish, you don't have to tell me. The mob scene isn't your bag. I'm going to look around tomorrow. Maybe find a couple of rooms to rent till I decide what to do."

I asked her what Sid thought about that.

"He thinks we should get an apartment together. But I'm not sure that's a good idea. What do you think?"

"Do you have to ask, Soph? You know my general outlook. You feel you can't get along without the man, okay. But if there's any doubt, skip it. Seems to me you're either passionately involved or en route to the nunnery. Why not take some time off?"

"You don't understand, Tish."

"Sure I do. I haven't always been seventy-something."

"Yeah, tell me about it." She kissed me goodnight. "No, don't you dare. I don't want to hear about anyone else's life. How easy everything was. How all the men in your life were perfect. How successful you—"

"Oh, go to bed. If I don't see you in the morning, give my love to the goats."

EIGHT

There was a functional problem when I tried to get out of bed the next morning. I was getting used to my sore tail and my livid arm hurt like hell, but I wasn't prepared for the stiff neck.

I knew from being the loser in bouts with animate and inanimate objects through the years that it was fatal to give in. So like an old drunk, I staggered into the bathroom and stood under the shower until I'd exhausted the supply of hot water.

Slathering on smelly Ben-Gay, I realized that the twist-and-dart action required to bite the brutal Treasury agent on the wrist must be the reason for my distress.

I brushed my teeth in a pensive mood. Never having bitten anyone before, I solemnly vowed never to do so again. Not only was the sensation of sinking my teeth into human flesh repugnant, but I was loathe to deepen my expensive relationship with my dentist.

Some sage has said that old age is when you do too many things for the last time and too few for the first. Guess I'm not as old as I thought.

I yanked out clean jeans and gingerly pulled on a cotton turtleneck. Bending over to tie my red sneakers wasn't easy.

Oatmeal laced with raisins and cinnamon gave me courage. Brewed Darjeeling perked up my spirits, and I downed a handful of vitamins that I hoped would help me through the day.

I taped a note for Sophie on the newel post and called Sue Rawby.

After a long wait, she said a brusque hello and started scolding me for having gone to the quarry so soon.

"Hey"—I held the phone away from my ear—"Hey! Help! Stop!"

When she wound down, I gave her a graphic description of my arm, and used other adjectives for my neck. "Bear in mind, please, that the demented public servant attacked me, not the other way around. But forget the encounter, Sue. What news? Have you lined up any suspects?"

Sue said there was nothing new and that if I insisted on drawing or painting at the quarry in the near future, to announce my intentions both at the business office and at the quarry. I didn't share the information that I planned to go to the quarry in a matter of minutes, but I did as Sue had instructed and telephoned the Ethan Allen office.

One of the secretaries summoned Wyman to the phone. He politely asked about my condition and told me he thought I would be foolish not to stay at home. He also said in response to my question that Sid had stepped out on business.

Once again I was overcome by the size of the quarry. We had been told the pit, as well as being twenty stories deep, was three-quarters of a mile long and more than a half mile wide.

The usual lumbering trucks, squeaking pulleys, and the chatter of pneumatic drills made it hard to believe that anything sinister could have taken place at this exposed and industrious workplace. With Lulu on a leash, I moseyed around trying to decide where to sketch, and finally settled on a spot near the sheds.

There was a tremendous temptation to sit safely in my roomy vehicle and not worry about rattlers, but that would defeat my objective, which was to be available to any and all comers who would talk to me.

My first visitor was my savior, Edgar Wyman. There was no talk about my being foolish. In fact, he treated me with a degree of deference. He told me his wife, Elvira, liked to paint. And he wondered if I minded if she came down and watched me.

I didn't much care about being watched but I'd deal with that when I met the woman. I told him I'd love to see her, and I meant it.

Wyman waved to a man walking by whom I recognized as the same person who had talked to Hilary and me the other day.

"Why don't you let Phil here show you what we do around here at Ethan Allen. I have to leave you."

From the minute Phil led me into the nearest shed, I felt I'd been dragged back into a Norman Rockwell *Saturday Evening Post* cover.

The ear-splitting whine of a huge diamond saw cutting through slate slabs that had been moved inside on rollers was so painful that I scurried past the eight-by-ten chamber with barely a glance. In the next room a handsome man, a reincarnation of the village smithy, was the sole occupant.

His bare torso covered by the bib of a heavy yellow apron took my breath away. The man wore gauntlets and in one hand he held a chisel and in the other a five-pound mallet.

The whole picture. A lumber company calendar askew on the sooty wall behind him, a lunch box featuring Mickey Mouse perched on the beam over the door, and that patch of yellow on his smooth olive skin. Wow! I wanted to park on a slate slab and pull out my paints.

After a moment of intense scrutiny, the gorgeous creature hit the slate slab a mighty blow. He seemed to be dissatisfied with the two sections he'd created and whacked it twice more, making four quite uniform chunks, which then rolled slowly along the track.

Yelling over the sound of the saw, I told Phil I thought slate split lengthwise, in thin pieces, like shale.

He nodded toward the next doorway. "It does in there. But we cut along the grain, too. Bill here's sculpting the stone."

In the next dark shed the foursome sitting on beat-up chairs or straddling stools could have been modeling for Rockwell's Spit and Chatter Club.

The men, all wearing gauntlets, grabbed Bill's sculpted slate and upended it on the dirt floor and, with hammer and chisel, split the stone into smooth slices. Phil described it as "splitting with the cleave."

After each piece had been severed from the slab, it was handed to another Rockwell character who whacked off a few rough edges and passed on the embryonic roof slate to another fellow who squared off the edges on a machine that may have predated the light bulb.

The shaped tiles were then piled on a hand trolley to be pushed over to the next shed, a hundred yards away. We followed.

Two cheerful men wearing caps, T-shirts, jeans, and, of course, gauntlets, stood in the eerie gloom of a high-roofed three-sided shed working at a machine Phil told me had excited a scout from the Smithsonian. The contraption was reminiscent of my grandmother's sewing machine stand. It was a fine example of the curlicue cast-iron era. Its purpose was to punch two holes in the top of each tile, a job that seemed to be accomplished by hand. I couldn't see if the hole puncher was activated by a foot pedal or if electricity had been introduced.

The older of the two men proudly demonstrated the process. He held a piece of slate on the machine; then he did press a foot pedal, causing a form to come down which punched out two holes. He then handed the slate to his fellow worker, who stacked the pieces against the wall or on a wooden flat.

It was easy to see why Sid had complained that the slate business was not the easy road to fabulous wealth. I knew that in the future I would look at slate roofs with new understanding and respect.

Whining saws in the next shed made me beg off on the extended tour. Phil pointed out the different colored slate stacked on skids all over the lot and told me that a large portion of their business was exporting as well as importing colored slate.

"Which ones are imported?"

"Over there, that black's from Spain and the green and black, that's from Norway. Our rock is over there." He pointed to dozens of racks of slate, some of which were being loaded by a forklift onto a truck. "It's nonfading slate—gray-green and purple. Color changes as you dig deeper. They'll be working this same pit one hundred and fifty years from now. Who knows what color it'll be then."

"Slate fades?"

"Oh, yeah. Some lower grades do. Turns sort of brownish. It freezes, too." Phil gestured toward huge chunks of rock sticking out of a long three-sided shed. "After it's been cut, it reacts to temperatures, and we gotta watch it until it's sculpted and split."

We crossed over a railroad siding Phil said wasn't being used much anymore. "We ship in cargo containers on flatbed trucks. It's all trucks nowadays."

"And this"—Phil pointed to a small building standing by itself—"is my favorite shop. It's where we make blackboards."

A grimy young man with a cigarette behind his ear was tossing a trowel full of sand over a revolving steel wheel.

"That's a rubbing bed," Phil enlightened me. While we watched, the young man depressed a lever, raising the top steel plate to examine the slick wet sheet of slate being sanded.

"A green blackboard?" I asked.

"Sure. That's our slate. We make 'em black, too, with stone from Pennsylvania."

Phil picked up a piece of chalk from a tool bench and wrote his name on a slab of slate leaning against the wall.

When he was done I used it to write TISH under PHIL. The temptation to add a heart around our names was strong. Instead I settled for drawing a frame, hanging from a triangle of wire from a nail that looked real enough to hit.

Just as we were leaving my eye caught writing on a slate behind us. NUMERO UNO IS A FUCKING FLIT.

Phil may not have seen it. I asked him as soon as we were outside what he thought of Sid. He shrugged, ignoring my question.

Before thanking Phil, I asked him if he was one of the people who had a key to the dynamite shed.

"Now I get to say 'no' for the forty-ninth time. NO. NO. NO."

This was said cheerfully and we parted chums.

I saw Wyman and Sid standing together as I rounded the corner of the blackboard house.

"Did Phil tell you," the foreman asked me, "that we keep the slate cozy and warm in those long sheds in the winter?"

Sid had folded his arms across his chest. He now raised his eyes in a classic expression of boredom and said, "Did you want something, Edgar?"

Horrified by Sid's rudeness I took Wyman's arm and twirled him around like a square dance partner and tucked my arm through his. Trying for a warm, chummy voice I told him that, yes, Phil had been an excellent and thorough guide. Wyman responded with a quick salute and disappeared into the nearest building.

Sid resumed his genial behavior. "Now, let's see," he said, rubbing his hands together, "how tough you are, Tish." He stepped in front of a gigantic truck lumbering toward us and raised his arm. "You game?" he asked.

Before I could reply Sid wrenched open the door, grabbed my waist from behind and, with what must have been his head under my bottom, catapulted me into the cab. The driver's three-fingered hand reached for mine and, with a brutal yank, pulled me up beside him.

"Holy Mary, lady. What's going on? You can't ride in this crate."

Sid straightened me up. As well as you can straighten up a doll with no stuffing. He didn't even greet the driver but told him to drive us down into the pit and after that to the repair yard. Whatever Sid may have said during our frightening tour went unheard by me. The straining engine roared like a furnace in Hades and any springs the ancient behemoth may have had were long since pulverized.

Sid almost wore out his index finger pointing out sights I could hardly bear to look at. Vertical drops below us and teetering mountains of rock above. I felt like a fragile pygmy at the bottom of the world's biggest manhole. I yearned for a sure-footed burro or a helicopter sling to take me back to my idea of solid earth. With grinding gears we finally did ascend and take our place among the derelict backhoes and tractors. It seemed like heaven.

None of the old trucks, Sid said, had to be registered because they never left Ethan Allen territory. He said his mechanics were geniuses. I wondered if the drivers were unlicensed too and remarked that the alcohol fumes emanating from our chauffeur had made me dizzy.

"Oh yeah," Sid said. "But don't worry, he usually gets there."

The most welcome wonderful sight was a woman walking toward us. She waved. It had to be Elvira Wyman, sprung from the rusted steel infirmary. I rushed to meet her. She was wearing a peaked cap. It had a message on the visor: JETS WIN.

"What do the Jets win?" I asked as we shook hands.

"Oh"—she took off the cap—"Forgot I had the silly thing on. It's my bowling club hat and the truth is we don't always win. I see Phil's been showing you around. It's no garden spot. I keep telling Ed he ought to paint some of these old sheds." She shrugged and smiled. "But it's hopeless."

Elvira's electric-blue sweatshirt seemed to match her metabolism. I had the feeling that if I had blown a whistle she'd be halfway to Poultney by now. The prospect of being watched by this wired woman didn't please me. But then I realized that my deceitful and sleazy reason for wanting to see her—to gather information—took precedence over pleasure.

"I do hope you're going to join me?" I asked as I pulled out a sketch pad. "I can lend you a pad, markers, whatever."

"Well, if you're sure you don't mind. I don't want to be a pest." She pointed. "Are those pastels?"

"Oil pastels. God's gift to artists on the run." I explained how simple it was to get an effect if one worked with the pastels on colored paper. I gave her a pale gray pad that I liked. "Back at the studio these sketches really have a punch. You know where you've been and with luck what to do about it."

Elvira quieted down as we both worked. Our conversation was sporadic and mostly about the upcoming library exhibition.

An hour may have passed before Elvira rose, stretched, and held up her picture. "I know this stinks."

It didn't stink. It was a bold and excellent impression of the slag piles behind the dynamite hut. I was able to admire it with sincerity.

"You left out the rattlers," I laughed nervously. Having been absorbed with my sketch, I'd forgotten I was standing on their turf.

"They won't hurt you if you don't get anywhere near them. Ed says he sees them mainly on the far side of the pit. Too many trucks around here. Not to worry about them."

Unzipping a canvas bag, I pulled out a wedge of cheese, a box of wheat crackers, and a plastic bag full of celery and carrot sticks.

Elvira demurred at first, but with Lulu's help we polished off the lot.

"I don't usually eat cheese. You know, cholesterol."

Kitty, I told Elvira, my next-door neighbor who was eighty-three and in good health, had a cholesterol count that hovered around four hundred.

With the purpose of my visit in mind, I asked Elvira if the little building made of cement blocks was where they kept the explosives.

"What a nightmare." She put her hands on either side of her face. Thus framed, she looked tired and older than the fifty years I'd first guessed. "That dynamite is a curse. I just wish they didn't have to use it all the time—and most of all, I wish Ed would learn that he can't get near the stuff. It nearly kills him."

"Kills him?"

"Lots of people get sick from dynamite. Not just when it explodes, but just smelling the sticks. Some of the guys here have to quit and go home after a detonation in the pit. Gives them awful headaches. I keep telling him, let the others handle the stuff. It doesn't bother the foreman or Norm. But like I say, it's going to kill Ed."

I expressed my concern and surprise about dynamite's side effects. I tried to remember, without success, if my head had ached when Sophie's house exploded.

"Ed's the worst. No one gets it as bad as Ed. Last week he was so sick he couldn't talk. My brother was visiting and he didn't even see him."

I couldn't let her wander. "His head ached last week?"

"Yeah. I don't even know what day it was. Oh yeah, Thursday. Poor Ed, he's been going through hell around here."

"You mean because of the explosion in Lofton? Or here?"

"Lofton. We often have minor accidents here; they don't need to be investigated."

Elvira talked about the invasion of police and people from the Treasury Department. How the disruption had brought all work to a stop. Ed, she said, was about ready to commit murder.

"Murder?" I asked cheerfully. "Who would he murder? Do you mean the T-men?"

"Ed told me about the one that grabbed you yesterday. That was awful."

I praised her husband's kindness and tried to bring the conversation back to the subject of murder.

"Maybe," I chanced, "maybe he'd like to murder the new owner of Ethan Allen. It must be very hard for your husband to have him show up. I've met the man and he seems quite, well, cocky."

"Cocky. Guess that's as good a word as any. This has been a wonderful time, Mrs. McWhinny. I can't wait to buy some oil pastels. And I love your little dog."

I was going to lose her. "Elvira, tell me. Who do you think took the dynamite and blew up Sophie Beaumont's house?"

She kept moving away. "I don't know. But I guess that's for others to decide." She paused. "I feel so sorry, Mrs. McWhinny. Especially now that I know you."

"Sorry?"

"Isn't Sophie Beaumont your niece?"

"Informally, yes. But listen, Elvira, if you're sorry about her house, don't be. The explosion was an awful shock. But the house—it was a rickety mess. I think we're all really glad it's gone."

"That's what I mean." She chewed her lip a second. "I mean it's your niece and Sid Colt. They're the ones that everyone thinks did it."

NINE

Walking home from Poultney would have been a good idea. I might have worked off some steam—steam generated by the thought that "everybody" could think that Sophie was a crook. That she would do anything as dishonest as destroying her own house for the insurance money. We hadn't discussed the dollar amount of insurance on her house, but I'd be surprised to learn that it was much more than ten or fifteen thousand dollars. Ten dollars or ten million dollars, it was inconceivable that Sophie could do such a thing.

To suspect Sid was different. It had occurred to me that he might have blown the place up so that Sophie would be homeless and make it easier for him to persuade her to move in with him. I acknowledged that the idea seemed a little far-fetched.

Edgar Wyman was my real suspect. I could imagine him framing Sid for the explosion. The man was so well shielded by his reasonable façade he might get away with the deed. But unimaginable crimes are committed in the name of jealousy every day, and of course I was thinking of what Elvira Wyman had told me about her husband's reaction to dynamite.

Driving well over the speed limit, I was lucky to have avoided a brush with the law in my eagerness to get to Lofton and to my telephone.

Sophie was stretched out on the living room couch reading a magazine. Lulu jumped on her stomach.

"Hey, you went to the quarry again without me." She sat up and looked at me more carefully. "You look kind of, well, threatening. What's up?"

There was no easy way of telling Sophie what Elvira Wyman said everybody thought. At the end of my recital of the morning's events, I repeated what everybody thought.

Sophie hit the ceiling. "Me, nuke my own house? Crazy fools!" She dashed into the library. "What's that 800 number? I've got it."

I filled the tea kettle and heard the exasperation in Sophie's voice as she talked to someone at the Treasury Department.

"They don't know where Sue Rawby is." She slammed down the phone. "They think she's away. They think! The assholes. And they run our government."

"That's not my favorite word."

"Assholes, right? How do you like dickheads?"

"I'm not crazy about the imagery in either case."

Quietly deflating, Sophie slumped on the kitchen table. "I get the feeling those jokers don't care. I think they're only interested in overseeing dynamite, and the hell with who does what with it. Think I'll call the detective I talked to that day."

I nodded in agreement, and even handed Sophie the Rockingham barracks number. I had planned to call the detective myself.

I felt so tired and blue I could have cried. Why did there have to be so many rotten mixed-up people in the world? There were probably thirty-five wars going on at any given moment, and more in the making. Hundreds of people were killed daily by vicious, careless, or misguided people, and now right here in beautiful Vermont, in safe serene Lofton, we had to face up to grim reality: that there was a deranged person, a criminal, with access to dynamite. I hugged Lulu and sighed.

Sophie reappeared after calling the detective.

"What's he like?" I asked.

She repeated my question. "Okay, nice. Laid back. Maybe a tiny bit blah. Has two pairs of glasses hanging around his neck and another perched on the top of his head. Name's Butler. I think."

"Oh, thought of something I forgot to tell you, dear." I described the blackboard shed and asked what she thought of the message: NUMERO UNO IS A FUCKING FLIT.

It was good to hear Sophie laugh. "Fucking's okay. Right? If flit means gay, I don't buy it. You know, you say yourself, Tish, that your eyes aren't so hot. I'll bet it said fucking shit. Sid's not the kid-gloves type or especially tactful, and you can imagine how much some of the guys resent him. Believe me, shit's the word."

"When will Butler be here? I've got to go to the store."

"He said within an hour. Come on. I need some things, too. We can see him from there."

What Sophie needed, aside from a tube of toothpaste, was an ice-cream cone, so she and Lulu sat outside on the bench to keep an eye out for Detective Butler.

Jake was alone in the store. "Mrs. McWhinny, I'm so glad it's you. Wanda and I have been talking to the others. We really feel it's time to move on and . . ."

"Move on? Do you mean leave Lofton? Leave the store?"

"Yes. Wanda has a sister in Miami. We're thinking of settling there."

I couldn't have been more surprised. Because some of us had minor misgivings about the Millers, it never occurred to me that they had doubts about Lofton and the store.

"I'm amazed, Jake. You've both said so often that you liked it here—even wanted to buy the place."

"Oh, I know, Mrs. McWhinny. Lovely people here. But things change and, well, that's just how we feel. We won't leave you in a spot or anything, but like I told the others, I hope you'll make plans, find someone else."

I leaned over the counter in a pose I hoped might invite an intimate disclosure.

"Is there any one particular reason for leaving, Jake? Something we might discuss and possibly iron out?"

For a minute I thought he might cry. He nibbled his lower lip.

"Tell me"—I leaned over and touched his arm—"tell me, Jake."

"Hello there, Mr. Walters," Jake greeted a customer. The moment had passed.

"Wait a minute, Mrs. McWhinny." He ducked behind the cold case and handed me a strip of pastrami. "For Lulu."

I told Sophie what Jake had said as we walked back to the house.

"Sid knows the Millers, remember I told you? Maybe he can get the story. But it's no big deal, is it, Tish? You're not all that crazy about them."

I admitted that that was true, but it just seemed such a lot of trouble finding someone new to run the place. Those of us who were responsible were a loosely gathered consortium and rarely in agreement.

Back home, Sophie vanished upstairs and I put the groceries away. In moments Lulu alerted me to Detective Butler's arrival. I had a chance to peek at him on the front porch before I opened the door.

He made me think of a heron as he stood first on one foot, then on the other as he polished the toe of each shoe on the back of a trouser leg. The general effect of a water bird was enhanced by his beaklike nose.

Because Detective Butler wore very dark glasses, I never did see the man's eyes—an unsettling feeling, like seeing only half a face.

Detective Butler's manner was friendly but solemn. Lulu got the picture and, after a quick sniff at his shiny shoes, joined Sophie and me on the couch.

"What I want to know," Sophie said, "is do you really suspect me of blowing up my own house?"

"It's not uncommon, Miss Beaumont, for houses that are beyond repair to be destroyed so that the owner can collect on the insurance money. But let me assure you, we have to consider every possibility and you have not been singled out as a suspect."

Slightly mollified, Sophie asked him whom he did suspect.

"We're still investigating." Detective Butler shrugged. "You wanted to tell me something?"

"You tell him, Tish."

After I described my morning with Elvira Wyman at the quarry and told him about her husband's allergy to dynamite, he spent some time tapping his front tooth with the end of his pen. Sophie's question went unanswered. He then brought up the subject of the dynamiter's blue car. The damn blue car. I could bring it clearly to my mind's eye but failed to see anything that would differentiate it from any other small blue car.

"Did you see Mrs. Wyman's car?"

"Yes. It was small, really small, and sort of off-white, and not at all the same shape as the blue car."

"And Wyman's car?"

"The day I went to the quarry with Hilary Oats I think I remember him getting into a pickup. But maybe that wasn't his car. Sorry to be so hopeless about these cars."

"Don't blame yourself, ma'am. If you live in the country, you've got to have a car and you can rent them, swap them, borrow and steal them. As often as not, a car turns out to be a very poor way of identifying a person.

"We have, of course, been questioning both Edgar Wyman and your friend Sid Colt. They appear to be the only two with access to the Ethan Allen dynamite supply who could have any connection to the situation.

"Your information about Wyman's allergy to dynamite may well be helpful, and we'll look into the matter."

Detective Butler closed his notebook, stood up, and cracked his knuckles. He admonished us to be wary and watchful, and he looked right at me when he said, "And keep an eye on that niece of yours."

"Stinker," Sophie said. "Me, I'm off to Goat Heaven. I'm going to clean the hell out of the barn."

I made myself spend the rest of the day in the studio. Usually I loved being in there, but my concentration level was zero.

I'd done a series of sketches of Sophie's goats, and a friend wanted to show them in her gallery. I hated to cut mats, but I managed to finish six decent-looking ones.

I don't really hate cutting mats. My beautiful old T-square pleases me, and my utility knives are always sharp. It was my inability to achieve a perfect beveled edge that got to me, but I'd long since convinced myself a straight cut looked just as good.

The next day I rehabilitated frames. Out of my assortment of frames I can never find the size of the painting or paintings I've just done, so I set up my mitre box equipment and cut wooden inserts that then had to be painted or stained.

I hadn't heard Sophie come in. "Tea, Tish?" Her offer was welcome.

"Please, I'm getting tired and careless, and the next thing you know I'll saw off my thumb."

"Anything good to eat?" Sophie was poking in the fridge. "Hey, where's Hilary?"

"Boston again. He should be back soon, anytime now."

"Soon!" She pointed at the bleating phone. "Right now, I'll bet that's Hil."

But it wasn't. An unfamiliar voice responded.

"Mrs. McWhinny, I'm Mary Spencer calling from Brattleboro Memorial Hospital. It's about Hilary Oats. He's been in an auto accident, but don't worry, he's fine. His condition is excellent. The police will inform you about the accident, something about a loose wheel. His car went over an embankment along the West River near Dummerston."

"When did this happen?"

"Day before yesterday."

"Good Lord, why wasn't I notified right away?"

"Mr. Oats requested that you not be told. He thought you'd worry and said you didn't expect to see him until today. He's very chipper, but asleep at the moment. You can call him a little later."

"That damned new car," Sophie moaned. "I knew Hil would have an awful time driving it. After the Beetle, I mean, has he ever driven anything else? But a loose wheel! I wonder how come?"

Detective Butler appeared at the front door and asked if he could come in. I guess I said yes. He found us sitting like zombies.

"I guess you've heard about Mr. Oats by now. I wanted to tell you at the time, but the M.D. asked me not to. Mr. Oats didn't want to frighten you."

"Please, Detective Butler, tell us exactly what happened," I said.

"I'm sorry to say that what happened does not appear to have been an accident."

Sophie and I both gasped.

He went on. "Officers at the scene think that it would be impossible for the wheel to have come off Mr. Oats's car unless the lugs had been deliberately loosened."

"Oh my Lord, I don't believe it." Sophie put her head in her hands. "I don't believe it."

"From your reaction to the news, Miss Beaumont, I take it you can't imagine that Mr. Oats has any enemies or greedy heirs."

"Of course he hasn't," I said. "And if he ever had any, he's outlived them all. My Lord, he's eighty-five."

"What about family?" Butler asked. "Any heirs—or anyone or some organization that is due to inherit his estate?"

"There's no one," I said. "Not a soul."

"Except me." Sophie pointed at herself. "He's leaving me his property. But don't even think what you may be thinking. I love the man."

"You didn't know about this, about your niece inheriting, Mrs. McWhinny?"

"Of course I did. It just slipped my mind. Why, he just told Sophie a couple of days ago."

"And his house?"

Sophie looked at me. "Is he leaving me the house? Gosh, I don't know."

Butler looked skeptical, or maybe that was his usual expression.

I said that Hilary's announcement of his plan to leave land to Sophie had been extremely informal and I doubted that there had been any discussion between them since that night.

"That's right," Sophie said. "I was overwhelmed and thanked him a thousand times. There were no details, not a word."

Excusing myself, I went into the library to call the hospital.

An ill-matched pair of rickety buildings blown sky high was one thing, but the thought that anyone would attempt to kill or even hurt Hilary made me sick.

I sank into Doug's old Morris chair. The glue that held my knees in place seemed to be missing and the eau de vie that kept me going was evaporating.

Lulu, always sensitive to my moods, was gazing at me myopically. We sighed in unison as I reached for the telephone book.

TEN

On the telephone, Hilary didn't sound like a fallen warrior. "Those damn cops, they expect to see a criminal behind every door. I told them, why would anyone want to do a thing like that to me? It was a dumb accident. I told them to go talk to Ed Bowers, where I bought the damn car. He probably has some nincompoop working for him who doesn't know a tire from a doughnut."

"The hell with the car, Hil. The important item—how are you?"

"My head's felt better, my left arm's felt better, and I think some giant socked me in the jaw. It's my disposition that's bad. Some teenage girl stationed here won't even let me go to the bathroom by myself. But the good news is the doctor says if I'm still alive tomorrow I can go home."

"Wonderful. I'll be there. What time?"

"After ten," he said. "A favor—please bring some pants and a clean shirt. When I was thrown out of the car I must have rolled in skunk scat."

Sophie came in as I put down the phone. "How is he?"

"Sounds fine. Grumpy. Wants me to bring him some clean clothes tomorrow."

"I'd offer to go pick him up but I have some people coming in the morning. They want to buy Tiffany's black-and-white kid as a pet. I know, why don't I go and get Hil's clothes for you right now, and maybe I should bring back Vanessa. She'll be lonely."

"Who's been feeding her? Hil didn't say anything to me."

"Sid."

"Sid! Your Sid? Our Sid? How did that happen?"

"Hil told Sid he'd be in Boston, and Sid really insisted he feed Vanessa, said he adored cats. I thought it was sweet."

"Well, I guess it was." What an old skeptic I'd become. It seemed clear to me that what Sid adored was Sophie, not cats.

No sooner had Sophie left on her helpful errand than Gray, calling through the door, announced his arrival.

I yoo-hooed from the kitchen and told him to come in. It wasn't easy. Pleasant as Gray was, what I wanted to say was bye-bye, nobody's home. The news of Hil's non-accident had been a real shock, and I needed repose and time to think.

Gray joined me in the kitchen. I watched him unconsciously lining up my unsorted flat silver on the counter, as he listened gravely while I told him about Hilary's misfortune.

With his eyes closed, Gray pinched the bridge of his nose. "I'm thinking. I'm trying to visualize Mr. Oats's car. Remember the other evening we went out to look at it? Well, you know what people do, men do, when they're inspecting a car. They kick the tires. I'll bet between us Sid and I kicked all four tires."

"Aren't the lugs hidden under the hubcap? You couldn't have seen if they were loose."

"That's what I'm trying to remember. I think I could see them. Oh well, I'm sure the police have been studying all that. What can I do to help?"

Gray might be a good chauffeur on the trip to Brattleboro the next day. Then I decided that there would be tiresome exit proceedings.

"Nothing, thanks. Sophie tells me I was less than polite about seeing your slides the other night."

"I was joking." He smiled. "Slide shows have almost gone the way of the button hook."

"You remember the button hook? Thought I was the only one." I asked him what he thought of Sid's pictures.

"Pretty good. But that talk about dealing with an Indian agent, good God. I hear they're all corrupt. I read somewhere that you can't even get a plumber or an electrician to come to your house without a liaison agent who arranges a bribe. Imagine what it's like in big-bucks business. Hope he knows what he's doing."

Envisioning Fair Haven and Poultney overrun with imported Indians, I asked Gray if Sid was really going to sell the quarry.

"He'd like to. Hope he has a savvy Indian tax lawyer."

"On his side, I hope. I . . ."

Whatever it was I hoped was lost when Sophie came running in the door. She didn't even greet us. Her eyes were as big as a china doll's and she held her hands in the air stick-up style.

"I'm scared. I'm scared!"

We both jumped up and clutched Sophie's arms as though we were trying to prevent her from levitating.

She shrugged out of our grips. "Come on—I'll show you. Hurry. No, not you, Lulu."

"Where?"

"Hil's. Hurry."

I followed the agile pair at a painful jog. The rough gravel on Hilary's road hurt my lightly shod feet.

What a relief when Sophie motioned us to stop, and drew our attention to an object on the ground.

Having dashed off without my glasses, I couldn't see a darn thing except the corner of a camera or box almost hidden by the leaves.

"What is it?" Gray knelt on the ground.

"Look at the wire." She pointed at a black wire coming out of the box and winding up the incline toward Hilary's house. "Whatever you do, don't touch it."

"I've got a nasty feeling," Gray said.

"Me, too." My eyes traced the wire up through Hil's defunct rock garden to where it disappeared under a clump of ivy. Walking cautiously, we followed the wire beyond the ivy, through the leaf-covered grass. We all stopped when we saw that the wire was attached to a soggy cardboard box.

"Dynamite." I don't know whether Gray or I uttered the word.

"I looked inside. That's what it looked like to me," Sophie said.

"Listen, both of you." Gray put a finger to his lips. "Hardly breathe. Wet dynamite is the most volatile thing in the world. A sneeze could set it off. When it's wet the glycerin turns into sulfuric and nitric acids or something and—just don't breathe. Tiptoe back."

Returning to the box downhill, Gray knelt on the ground. "This has batteries in it, I guess. It's the detonator. Oh, boy." He reached out and took Sophie's hand for a second. "I'm glad you're all in one piece. I don't dare touch this thing. I'll stand guard here. You call the Treasury people and the police. Tell them to hurry. Looks like a storm brewing, and lightning could—"

"We're not apt to have an electrical storm in the fall," I said.

"All we need is a one-volt bolt on Stratton and it's curtains. For God's sake, hurry."

Sophie shot off like an Olympic sprinter and I followed at a spiritless trudge with a heavy, troubled heart.

Who would want to hurt Hilary? I made myself face it out loud. Kill Hilary. My loving chum, that monolith of decency. I couldn't imagine anything he was capable of doing that could invite such evil. His growl was amiable. His social targets were not unusual and were rarely personal. I was biased, of course, but it seemed to me he went out of his way to be fair and generous. There had to be some other reason.

That's what Sophie said when I made it to the house five minutes behind her, kicked off my espadrilles, and fell into the wing chair.

She was lying on the couch with Lulu sitting in her usual place, on Sophie's stomach. "Hil has no enemies. There must be another reason. It's insane."

"Insanity. I guess it's a possibility, but not probable."

"You know what I'm thinking, Tish, and so are you. Someone wanted him dead to get his place. Like, what else has he got? And who will benefit? Me! So I practice by nuking my own house, then plan to blow up his." She sat up and hugged Lulu. "Someone's crazy. I hope it isn't me."

"You called, of course."

"Of course. Got Sue right away. I mean, she nearly hyperventilated. Said as soon as you got back I was to go out and stand on the road. Make sure no one drives up Hil's road."

When she went to the door, I followed. "We can see his road from the porch. Wait a minute. What else did she say? What's next?"

"She'll try to get the bomb squad truck from Albany or Boston, so you better stay inside by the phone in case she calls. Is this some kind of a nightmare?" Shaking her head, Sophie walked up the road. Charlie stopped her in front of the post office. I watched his gestures of surprise, then the classic wringing of hands. He massaged one of his Mickey Mouse ears as he talked earnestly, then they walked toward Hilary's together.

Good for Charlie, I thought. Sue had assigned Sophie a spooky job.

I was back inside when the phone rang and a woman calling for Agent Sue Rawby told me that the bomb squad coming from Albany would arrive in about two and a half hours, but that Sue would be in Lofton shortly.

Lulu didn't like being closed up in the kitchen, but with so much going on I had a horrible vision of her slipping out the door to find Sophie.

I closed the door in the nick of time. A state trooper knocked on my door just as the phone rang. It was Hilary. They couldn't find his shoes. He wanted me to bring his brown loafers. I knew he'd probably have a heart attack if he knew what was going on.

"Okay, okay, dear. I have to run. Come in, officer," I called.

"Ma'am, we have orders to evacuate this part of the village. They're opening the church."

"Forget it, officer. Look, the church is right next door. I'm staying here."

Sue Rawby opened the door. "It's all right, officer. I'll take over. Your lieutenant's outside."

Before I could even speak to Sue, Sophie came, with Gray

tagging along, and everyone gathered on the porch.

Sue congratulated us for being alive. "We have no way of knowing how long the dynamite's been in place. It's a miracle that nothing has happened."

"Are you okay, Tish?" Sophie had seen something in my face that I just felt in my throat. I was going to be sick.

With a long arm around my waist, she propelled me into the library and just in time shoved me into the bathroom.

Cast iron is the way I've always described my stomach. I guess age was catching up with me. Or maybe it was my imagination. The thought of Hilary shattered, torn apart like Sophie's linoleum, made me sick. I couldn't stand around and talk as though the possibility of Hil's being splattered to death was some lively town event.

I said as much to Sophie when she came in. "My imagination is too gory and graphic and . . . oh my Lord, Vanessa!"

Sophie was gone before I finished saying the cat's name. I tore after her. "She's going to get the cat," I yelled.

For about two seconds, everyone on the porch was frozen. Then as though I'd shot off the starting gun, they sprinted after Sophie. None of them caught her. I doubted anyone could, but the troopers stationed by Hilary's road did, and it wasn't easy.

It was a wild scene, with all the troopers and the sprinters trying to pacify frantic Sophie. What a tragedy if the dynamite could be set off by Sophie's voice calling her captors fucking dickheads. Sue seemed to be the soothing agent, and with Gray on Sophie's other side, the trio returned to my house.

I retired to the kitchen with Lulu and filled the kettle for tea and coffee. Gray opened the door and peeked in. "May I?"

"Please, please. But close the door. I don't want to be surrounded. How's Sophie?"

"She's okay. I think she likes the agent."

"And you? How are you bearing up?" I patted his bony shoulder and automatically picked off some Lulu hair. I should put a sign on my front door: LEAVE YOUR DARK CLOTHING ON THE PORCH.

"Nothing's wrong with me," he said. "I just wish the bomb truck would come."

"I'm rather surprised, Gray, that you haven't packed up and said goodbye to Lofton now that your favored tract of land isn't available." I softened my curiosity by adding that we all were very glad he was still here.

"There must be a little Scottish blood in my veins. I paid Fay for three months and wouldn't think of leaving until my time is up. Besides, who wants to leave Vermont at the most beautiful time of the year?"

He didn't mention Sophie's attractions and I was in no mood for a discussion of Gray's amorous expectations, so I changed the subject and confessed I was eager to see the bomb squad's rolling fortress.

Just as the light was fading, the truck arrived. It didn't look like just any truck. Each side was covered with a chain blanket, with links as big as my fist. The superstructure shapes suggested a hoist or crane. We watched the odd vehicle stop beside the police car, and three men got out and proceeded to dress in outer-space costumes, modern-day armor.

"We can see Hil's house from the blueberry clearing." Sophie reached up on the bookcase where I kept a pair of binoculars. "It will be safe. Come on."

It would be something to do instead of keeping our miserable vigil on the porch. No one was paying any attention to us, so we took off through the back door.

Gray and Sophie waited for me along the path and lent an occasional hand, but I was glad when we got there. My heart was pounding and I wondered, as I had from time to time, if I had been taking Lulu's pills and giving her mine. Our look-alike pills sat side by side on a kitchen shelf. Lulu's were for asthma and mine were baby aspirin that *The New York Times* told me to take.

The guard was getting out of the truck; we could see it clearly. An arm from the top of the truck moved over to the box—at least I assumed it was the box of dynamite—and I think we all held our breath as a padded claw came closer and closer. The men moved behind the truck as the claw retrieved the soggy box. It took forever for it to lift the dynamite into the rear opening of the truck and another eternity for the claw to resettle itself above. It took even longer for the men to search the rest of Hil's property.

With just the driver inside, the truck moved like molasses, and left our field of vision.

Once again Sophie was the leader, and we went down the well-worn path to Hilary's house.

ELEVEN

"There you are." Sophie hugged Vanessa. "Look, she must have known something was wrong; she's all jittery." The cat leapt out of Sophie's arms and ran into the kitchen.

"Maybe she smelled the dynamite," said Gray. "Or maybe her sixth sense is at work. Can I help you do anything, ladies? Otherwise, I'll take off."

We assured him no help was needed and he left, promising to call Sophie the first thing in the morning.

"I don't know when Ruth is supposed to come, but soon, I hope. It smells horrible in here."

"Before we're visited by all the fuzz, the agents, truck drivers, and whoever else is in town, let's get Hil's clothes." Sophie counted on her fingers. "Shoes, socks, pants, shirt, and maybe a sweater or a jacket."

"Whew, Hil's going to have a fit when he hears about this."

"A fit? I doubt it. He'll probably think someone planted the dynamite just for something to do on a lazy afternoon."

I marched into Hilary's bedroom. Two enormous maple trees

on the south side of his bungalow kept the room in leafy dusk. I flicked on the light switch.

I don't know how long I stood there. Maybe just seconds until Sophie nearly knocked me down, pushing by me to fall on her knees beside Sid's folded body. He was rounded over in a head-to-knee pose, and at Sophie's tremulous touch his body rolled over like a boulder, knocking over the bedside table and a brass lamp that landed on his shoulder with its shade coming to rest on his head like a Halloween hat. Flies rose from beneath it.

I watched water from Hilary's fallen thermos pitcher join the huge stain on the Navajo rug. Sid's orange turtleneck sweater made the dried blood look like rust. His usually robust color had seeped away, and his profile stood out against the dark red background like bleached driftwood on a carpet of seaweed.

A sound of mortal anguish rose from Sophie. "Oh dear God, dear God, what happened?"

I leaned over Sophie and put my arm around her. "Up. Come on, get up, dear." I led her out of the room and sat her down beside the telephone. Tears streamed down her face and the sounds she made sounded like a lonely puppy.

Hoping to catch the police, perhaps at my house, I dialed my own number with no luck. But the Rescue Squad did answer and I told them about Sid and said I knew they couldn't move him until he was pronounced dead by a doctor, so I asked them to call one. I felt Sophie shudder. At the police barracks I left word for Detective Butler. I hoped they could catch him before he got too far from Lofton.

I drew over a chair and held Sophie's hand. With my eyes closed I had no trouble seeing the murder scene. I wondered if Sophie had noticed Hilary's fire poker beside Sid's body. The poker he was so proud of. The poker he'd made himself.

Sophie, her eyes closed, was now shivering. Would a shot of brandy help, I wondered. Or an aspirin—the pill I took for everything that ailed me. Hilary scorned pills and if he had any, they'd be in the bathroom cabinet. I wasn't about to go back through the bedroom. I covered Sophie's shoulders with a huge woolly cardigan Hilary had left over the back of a chair.

While we waited quietly I guess I murmured inanities. My thoughts were in a tizzy. Dynamite and loosened lugs were the tools of a remote murderer, but a hands-on killer, a deliberate maniacal attack on another human being—right here in Hil's house!

"Vanessa." Sophie looked more like herself. "If Vanessa could talk, what would she tell us? I guess it's got to be that manager, you know. But kill Sid? Insane."

Once again we lapsed into silence until lights appeared and we heard cars stopping on the gravel. We stood up, automatically squaring our shoulders.

Carol Zimmer, one of the stars of our wonderful Rescue Squad, was the first person in the door. She simply said, "Where?"

I pointed to Hilary's bedroom. She was followed by a couple of teammates with a stretcher. Within minutes, a state trooper appeared and followed them. Next, Detective Butler rushed by us. How the man could see with those dark glasses was beyond me. I figured he was following his nose.

Sue Rawby showed up next. She put her arm through Sophie's. "What happened?"

"Someone murdered Sid, killed him, in Hil's room." Sophie hid her face with her hands.

Sue turned to me. "I was talking to Butler outside the drugstore in Londonderry when this came over the wire. Thought maybe I could help." She nodded in Sophie's direction. "She's had a rough day."

Not nearly as rough as it became with the detective's questioning a little later.

After the arrival of Dr. Wolf, who told us what we all knew—that Sid was dead—he said that from an educated guess, Sid had been murdered sometime yesterday and that death appeared to have been caused by a blow at the base of the skull by the poker at his side.

Bob Wolf was a lively young friend and very able practitioner. He said, "I can only attest to his demise. Whatever else I said has to be verified by the experts." He gave Sophie a hug. "Sorry, my dear. I hear you two were close. Call me if you need anything. Bye."

Whatever they were doing in Hilary's bedroom seemed to take forever. Sophie and I both sighed with relief when Detective Butler dashed out in response to the next crunch of tires. He ushered in a washed-out young blond woman with shoulders barely wide enough to hold up her array of cameras and lights.

I wasn't sure she even saw Sophie and me until a flash bulb momentarily blinded us.

"In here." Butler steered her into the bedroom and paused to tell us that we were lucky: Nancy, the crime unit photographer, had been located nearby. The homicide van, he assured us, would arrive soon.

When we heard the van arrive, Sophie and I went into the kitchen with Vanessa. I didn't want to see or greet the ghoul experts and technicians.

While I drink for pleasure, not survival, I had a feeling this might be a time to yank out Hil's single-malt Scotch. While I was halfway in the armoire, I got out some Calvados for Sophie, who was leaning on the kitchen counter, her arms around Vanessa, softly crying.

It's good Hilary couldn't hear Sophie say "yuck" as she gulped down his precious brandy.

"Tish, who would want to kill Hilary as well as Sid? I mean, like what's the connection—and why, why, why?"

Detective Butler looked in. "We're waiting for Mr. Gray. When he comes we'll try to sort things out."

He ducked out before I could ask any questions. I could see him talking to Sue Rawby and one of the homicide squad people.

"Oh God, I can't look." Sophie moved away from the door. Carol was leading her group out of the bedroom.

"Carol," I called. "You're not taking Sid. Why . . . ?"

"Nope. We've called the hearse. Sorry about your friend. No one could have survived that blow. Hey. Sophie, I'm really sorry."

Even though I knew he was gone . . . the hearse. How terminal. An ambulance made anything seem possible. Dedicated people and medical miracles at work. But a hearse is so final. Hope lost.

Sue joined us and tried to explain the trying pace of the investigation. "The integrity of a murder scene is vital. The murderer often leaves something, takes something, moves something important for a reason that may be fathomed later. It's slow going, but I think they're almost finished."

Minutes later Gray appeared. He looked hesitant greeting Sophie. Probably he wanted to hug her, too, but settled for clasping her hand in both of his and saying something I couldn't hear. He did tell us both that Detective Butler wanted us all in the living room.

Butler, Sue, and a trooper sat at the refectory table. They all had notebooks at the ready. I joined them. Gray and Sophie sat together on the couch.

"About the dynamite," Sue said. "Just want to tell you that it is en route to a place where it can be turned into inert matter or detonated. And Detective Butler agrees that it would be suitable to ask you, Sophie and Mr. Gray, to repeat your experiences with dynamite."

"Mrs. McWhinny, I want to ask you"—it was the detective's question—"how long was your niece gone when she found the dynamite?"

I looked at Gray. We both shrugged. "Ten minutes, more or less."

"And what did you do during that time, Miss Beaumont?"

"I was going to get some clothes for Hilary when I saw the black box, then the wire. I followed it up and looked in the carton. I figured it was dynamite."

"That took ten minutes."

"If Tish says so."

"I see. Just wanted to ask you. The tennis tournament the other day in Dorset. Did you win?"

My slight smile at the silly question became rigid when Sophie didn't answer.

"Dear, Detective Butler asked you about—"

"I know. I heard him." Sophie looked everywhere but at Butler. Rather like a child looking for an escape route. "I should have told you. I forgot."

It was hard, but I kept quiet. You could hear the proverbial pin drop.

"What happened was . . ." Sophie paused a long time. "Well I bashed into this dumpster in Manchester and my bumper jammed into my tire and I had to get it fixed before I could drive it. I felt so stupid I thought I might as well keep it to myself. Then my house, you know, exploded, and I just forgot all about it."

Expelling the breath I didn't know I was holding, I chirped something about how understandable it all was.

Detective Butler's dour expression made it clear he didn't share my feeling.

"Miss Beaumont, do you mean that with all the discussion and all the questions posed about the dynamiting of your house, you thought that withholding the truth might not be a serious offense?" He shook his head in wonderment.

"It was dumb, I guess," she said. "But I didn't think it was important."

"I'll remind you that after Mr. Oats's near fatal car episode you also forgot"—he slathered the word "forgot" with sarcasm—"you also forgot that you were the sole heir to this place and to the rest of his property." His broad gesture suggested that Hil owned all of Lofty Mountain.

Sophie looked down at her entwined fingers. Gray protectively moved closer. "I'm sorry, it's true. I just forgot. But just for a minute."

"Another question. At any time have you and the deceased discussed what you would do with your inheritance? Possibly the deceased wanted to share it with you."

The insulting suggestion transformed Sophie from her passive state into a raging tigress. She almost knocked the detective out of his chair as she strode over and stuck her face within inches of his. "Here," she snarled as she hit his shoulder hard with her fists. "You'd better handcuff me right now, or I'll beat you to a pulp."

I'm sure no one, including Butler, doubted that she could do it. I think everyone was relieved when she straightened up and pulled back her unmanacled wrists.

"Do you really think I'd blow up my very own house—try to kill Hilary and murder Sid?"

"This is all ridiculous." Gray stood up. "Certainly anyone in his right mind would know that Sophie Beaumont had nothing to do with any of these awful events. And murder? Good God!"

Sue raised her hand and spoke, quietly defusing the situation. "Tell us what, if anything, happened, Mr. Gray, while you were guarding the detonator and the wire and the path to the dynamite."

"Nothing, really. I spoke to one of the troopers who came up. He said he'd take my place, but so far he'd just had orders to guard the driveway. When he left, Jake Miller went by. I didn't talk to him; I motioned him away. He looked pretty puzzled, but he left. Then someone relieved me. That's all. I kept looking out for Mr. Oats's cat, but I didn't see it."

Butler asked him if he knew Edgar Wyman, and Gray said yes, they'd met and had talked some on another occasion when Sid invited him to the quarry. "And I take it you didn't see him." Gray shook his head.

"We are, for the moment, assuming that the deceased was killed sometime during the day yesterday. I'd like to know what you were doing. Why don't we start with you, Mrs. McWhinny?"

I told him I'd been working in my studio the last two days, with people drifting in and out. And I assured him a bit sarcastically that I had plenty of time to go up to Hilary's undetected, but that I didn't think I was physically capable of committing such a brutal murder. I didn't like Butler. I didn't like his holier-than-thou attitude and I most emphatically didn't like the way he was picking on Sophie. Maybe it was those feelings that made me ask him if he had decided who had almost killed Hilary by loosening his lugs.

"Not yet." He didn't even look at me when he replied. "I think we'll find all of these events—Miss Beaumont's explosion, Mr. Oats's loosened wheel, the dynamite planted here at his house, and the murder of Sid Colt—are all connected."

Both Sophie and Gray, under Butler's ponderous quizzing, gave hopeless accounts of their activities for the last two days. They had been all over the place doing different things and rarely connected with anyone who could provide an alibi— except for me. They both had been in and out of my house but I had no idea when or what time or which day.

"Mr. Gray, did you know the deceased?"

"Yes, I did. Mr. Oats introduced us."

"You didn't know him in India?"

Gray shook his head. "Nope. Never been there."

Butler folded his notebook. He said he knew that all of us would not leave the area and would be willing to make ourselves available at any time.

I walked back into the kitchen to put my empty glass in the sink.

"Just wanted to say goodbye." A smiling Detective Butler held out his hand.

Shaking his hand, I couldn't resist a comment on his cheerful demeanor. "If I may say so, you look downright happy."

"Happy? Not really. Almost, though." He leaned against the counter, and in a quiet voice with words intended just for my ears, he said, "Murder is a terrible thing, ma'am, terrible. Most murder victims are killed in squalid circumstances by their husbands, wives, lovers, and friends, or by the landlord or a lunatic, and everybody knows who did it. In fact, as often as not, the murderers call and tell us about it. Murders that are mysteries are few and far between, and they challenge us. Yes, make us almost happy. It's a puzzle you've got to solve. Like, I didn't know the victim. I'm sorry for your niece, but there isn't a weeping wife or sad children, so my main objective is to find the killer and bring him, or her, to justice. You want to know terrible? You want to know awful? Abuse, that's what's terrible. Especially child abuse. I've never met a cop that didn't feel dirty just talking to one of them. Never knew a cop who didn't want to strangle an abuser—yeah, even murder 'em. Now that's unhappy work."

Butler's heartfelt recitation about his feelings surprised me. I was almost sorry that he'd revealed that he was a regular decent human being. It was easier to regard him as a symbol of the law who might or might not be helpful. But before I could really like the man, he'd have to take off those damn dark glasses.

When Butler said goodbye to me and the others and promised we'd be seeing a lot more of him, I knew I could believe it.

Sue and the state trooper left at the same time. Gray followed them out the door.

This was the first time I'd ever felt frightened and miserable in Hilary's funny, funky old bungalow.

TWELVE

Sophie returned from saying goodbye to Sue with a fistful of mail. "Hil's." She waved it at me. "Charlie must have brought it up." Hilary and I both had boxes at the post office, but when they were overloaded, helpful Charlie would deliver the mail himself.

Throwing the mail on the table, Sophie paced around the room and in and out of the kitchen while I collapsed on Hilary's gigantic lumpy couch. "Don't let that Butler gent get to you, dear. He'll simmer down by tomorrow."

"Sid won't be any less dead tomorrow, and damn it, Tish, somebody killed him. You didn't, I didn't, Gray didn't, Charlie didn't, the Millers didn't—and who else in Lofton knew him? It has to be Edgar Wyman."

"But that seems so far-fetched. So Wyman blew up your house to frame Sid. Then he tried to kill Hilary. Why? Then he murders Sid. Why? Seems crazy, but maybe the man's obsessed. Although we mustn't forget that if Wyman hated Sid, maybe everyone who worked in the quarry felt the same way." I almost reminded her about the sentiment about Sid I'd seen on the blackboard, but thought better of it. "And, too, dear, how about all the people he met with you? He did have a rather aggressive personality."

"That was all front, Tish."

"Maybe. How about the deals he talked about? Indian agents, and Lord knows who else. I wish I had more faith in Butler."

Befuddled is not a word I like to apply to myself, but it fit my condition. I couldn't seem to concentrate on all the horrors. I was incapable of sorting things out, of singling out one event and examining it. I felt as though I'd turned on a scrambled television station.

In the next second I lost what slight grip I had on reason and sanity.

The first intimation of the ghastly episode to come was tactile. Something moved under my hand. Something cool and rounded seemed to flow like a hose under my fingers. I yanked my hand back from between the seat cushions. Then I saw the snake, or part of it. Neither its head nor tail was visible, but a portion of its mud-colored body looked as thick as my forearm.

When I jumped to my feet, Sophie must have heard me gasp or yelp and dashed in from the kitchen. Vanessa leapt out of her arms, landed on Hilary's table, and hissed.

With our backs to the wall, we watched the monstrous reptile reveal itself. Its wedge-shaped head appeared first, waving from side to side; its tongue darted in and out.

"I don't think they can see," Sophie whispered.

"They sense body heat, I think." And at that moment, my temperature was a hundred and ten.

Slowly the creature coiled itself on the cushion. Its knobbed tail was the last part of its anatomy to surface.

Mercifully my poor eyesight spared me from counting its rattles. An inch at a time, Sophie moved toward the telephone by the front door.

Vanessa's display of anger or fright worried me. I was afraid she'd provoke the snake. So I slid over to the table, and, with her clutched in my arms, joined Sophie, who had already dialed the number.

"Jake." Sophie identified herself. "I've heard you know about snakes. Aunt Tish and I are at Hilary Oats's house, and there's a huge rattlesnake on the couch. Oh? It's Wanda who knows about snakes? Hi, Wanda. How far? Tish, how far are we from the snake? I guess fifteen feet. Okay, Wanda, we will. Thanks. And hurry."

Sophie hung up abruptly. "She said not to move."

Rattlesnakes are tough, death-dealing reptiles, and there's good reason to be afraid of them, but even if our rattler had been a harmless black snake, I'd still be repulsed and have the shivers. The snake flicked its tail, which seemed to activate the rattling process. Then it vibrated so intensely it became a blur.

Poor Vanessa. I nearly had to strangle her to keep her from leaping out of my arms.

"I think he's got six rattles," Sophie said.

"Oh dear." I suggested maybe we could sneak out the front door, but Sophie stood firm.

The bizarre image of Wanda Miller as a herpetologist was almost replacing my fear.

"How did you know about Jake—I mean Wanda."

"Some little kid who found a snakeskin told me. Maybe Sid did, too."

Just saying his name shattered Sophie's brave composure, and tears streamed down her cheeks.

We stood in silence, mesmerized by the venomous reptile.

When Wanda came through the door, she appeared to have grown in stature, and her eyes glowed. Wimpy whiny Wanda looked like St. Joan. She wore hip-high waders, jeans, and a leather jacket. In one hand she held a forked stick that looked like a slingshot. In the other hand she carried an assortment of paper and plastic bags and a bath towel. A camera hung around her neck.

"What a beauty," she exclaimed. "It's got to be three feet long, maybe more. And thick, wow! Never seen one that color. You're seeing a rare species—a real live Vermont timber rattler." Wanda put her equipment on the table and, crouching down, brought the camera to her eye.

The rattler didn't share Wanda's enthusiasm for their meeting and seemed very agitated. I wanted to run out the door but was stopped by the memory of an illustration in an important book of my childhood. The graphic picture showed a snake with its tail in its mouth, forming a hoop, and rolling down the road after a doomed child. I could see such a ghastly scene with me, the victim, racing down Hilary's driveway.

How far could a rattler strike? Or did its venom fly through the air? Fearless Wanda with her camera on the ready had been inching closer and closer to the snake. I guessed her to be about ten feet from the deadly beast, which was rattling its tail off and opening and closing its jaws in an ominous fashion. For a moment I thought Wanda was going to ask the snake to say "cheese." When the camera flash went off, the snake dropped to the floor with a thud and, looking like molasses ribbon candy, made for Hilary's bookcase.

No cold-blooded creature could have chosen a more perfect retreat—the bottom of Hilary's vast bookcase, which was made up of stacks of papers, both in and out of binders, piles of magazines and newspapers, tattered paper folders, and dog-eared account books. Snake heaven. Warm cozy insulation and plenty of mice for dinner.

I thought we'd never see the snake again, in which case it would be the last time I'd ever be found in Hilary's house. However, I'd underestimated Wanda, who flushed out the reptile in seconds and, on a zig-zag course, followed him across the floor. I considered fainting but was too gripped by the scene. In one deft movement, Wanda tossed her towel over the reptile.

"It confuses them," she said.

We watched as Wanda pounced on the inert towel. She grasped what must have been either end of the snake and called for a brown paper bag. "Hey, hurry—he's strong."

I didn't move a muscle. Sophie looked doubtful, but moved quickly and put an open brown sack within a plastic bag beside the towel. She stepped back just as quickly.

Wanda dropped the snake, still hidden by the towel, into the bag. She held it closed and slipped a rubber band off her wrist and secured the top.

She was elated. "What a specimen. You know, there are hardly any rattlers around here anymore. It's too cold. They don't like the winters any more than I do. Or the fall, or the cold spring. They're an endangered species. Did you know that?"

The rattler looked just fine to me—full of beans and lively. I felt like the endangered species. "How did you become such an expert—so knowledgeable about snakes?"

"Ask Sid. We had lots of snakes near where we lived. Mainly copperheads, but some rattlers too. There was a bounty on them then, and we thought nothing of killing them. But now it's different. I feel I've got a real prize. Crazy, isn't it?"

"Wanda," I said, "you don't know about Sid. He's dead. He was murdered right here. In the bedroom. The police have just left."

Wanda nearly sat on the rattler, which she had casually put back on the couch. She didn't say anything for quite a while.

"You were good friends?" I asked.

"We grew up together." She paused. "I saw the Rescue Squad and wondered where it was going. I have to get back." She jumped to her feet.

She went toward the door, pausing to touch Sophie's arm. I thought she was going to speak, but instead she rushed on outside.

"Hey!"—I was galvanized into action—"You forgot the snake!"

Wordlessly she dashed back inside, retrieved her prize with no more care than if it had been a bag of popcorn, and ran outside again.

I sank onto the telephone chair and handed Vanessa to Sophie. "Poor thing's tired of being strangled. We'd better take her with us."

"You know what they say about snakes, Tish."

I didn't want to know but I tried to look receptive.

"They usually have a mate."

"Oh, my Lord. I wonder if I'll ever be able to sit on that couch again. I don't even want to go into Hil's bedroom again, but I've got to get those clothes." The errand took me seconds. "Let's go. I think I'd rather have a nervous breakdown at home."

It was pitch-black out, so we took Hilary's big torch off its hook by the door. Tending our own thoughts, we walked home. Vanessa and Lulu greeted each other by touching noses and tore out into the kitchen. Sophie and I went to our rooms. I soaked in the tub, and Sophie, I gathered from her appearance an hour later, had mourned for Sid.

She found me in the library, a Scotch and soda in one hand and my other resting on the telephone.

Hilary had to be told about Sid right away. I knew how fast sensational news traveled and I wanted to soften the blow. How do you soften the blow of an attempt on your life and property with dynamite and a murder in your own bedroom? It wouldn't be easy.

Once again I asked Sophie about Sid's friends or family.

"He had no family. You heard him, his ex-landlady forwarded mail."

"You'll be asked, you know, and soon, about a service of some kind. That's what funerals are for. It's make-busy time so you can perform, not think."

She said his only family connection she knew of was his uncle's lawyer, who had told him about inheriting the quarry. "But Sid says he's out of it. Had a stroke, and may even be dead, for all I know. And he mentioned George. That was his friend in India who's in New York."

"How do we get hold of him?"

Sophie shrugged. "Dunno. Sid said he lived in Greenwich Village. I'll talk to Wanda and Jake. Maybe they know something I don't."

There was a knock on the door, and Sophie let Gray in. He said he'd been thinking about us and maybe he could take us out for a quiet dinner.

"That's sweet of you, Gray. Sophie can speak for herself, but count me out. That damn rattlesnake siphoned off my last ounce of vitality."

"Rattlesnake? Good God, where . . . ?"

Sophie told him.

"The rotten son of a bitch!" he said.

"I don't know who you mean," Sophie said. "But Wanda was really wonderful. What a savior."

"Who's an SOB, Gray?" I asked.

"Whoever brought the snake to Mr. Oats's house."

Befuddled was the right word for me. So much had gone on in the last hour I hadn't given a thought to who had introduced the rattler to Hilary's house. I guess, without thinking, I assumed it had come down from the mountain and was somehow just there.

"Have you reported this to the detective?" Gray asked.

I shook my head. "I haven't got what it takes."

"I'll do it, Tish, and we'll see if old dickhead thinks I did that, too," Sophie said.

Gray and I talked while Sophie called Butler on the kitchen phone.

"Gray, do you think it was Sid or Wyman who brought that rattler to Hilary's? The quarry's just about the only place you'd find a rattler in Vermont."

"Who knows?"

"Well, who do you think killed Sid?"

Gray shrugged and held up empty hands. "The only person I can think of who would benefit from his death is Wyman— but murder's a pretty severe reaction to the possibility of losing your job."

"Severe, I'll say; but you read about it all the time. Disgruntled employee shoots boss."

"I talked to Sid yesterday—or was it the day before? Did you know? He sold the quarry. That may have been the last straw for Wyman."

That Sid had sold the quarry was the first piece of news I'd heard that wasn't vicious or depressing, so I urged Gray to tell me more.

He said he didn't know much except that Sid had been very pleased with the deal. He'd sold it through the agent he met in Nassau to that Indian company, and Ethan Allen had made some kind of swap of assets that would avoid taxes. "The money, Sid said, would go into an account in the Bahamas, so zero taxes." Gray didn't know the price but he estimated about four or five million.

"How do you think the Indians will take to Vermont?" Sophie, who had come in while Gray was talking, asked the question.

"Maybe there won't be any Indians. They wanted Sid to stay on and run the quarry. What happens now I don't know. Sid wanted me to join the company, but I'm not willing to work that hard."

"Gray, you and Sid certainly became friends very quickly, which, I must confess, surprises me. He acted so possessive about Sophie, and you clearly enjoy her company, too."

"Well, yes, there is that. But Sid was all business; we never even discussed Sophie. He knew I'd had a lot of experience in the computer world—and you know, communications are going to take off. The whole field's jumping up and down on a springboard. He thought I might be just the person he wanted; so he talked to me about his plans for the quarry. But as I told you, I really didn't want to take on a consuming job. Didn't— and don't. But I'll tell you what I am willing to do." Gray's face lit up. "I think I'll buy the store."

"What store?"

"Here. The Lofton store. Your store."

"I didn't know it was for sale," said Sophie. "Is it, Tish?"

"Well, yes and no," I hedged. "There are quite a few of us who have to decide that question. But Gray, if you think running the store isn't hard work, you've got a guess coming."

"Oh, I wouldn't work there. I'd hire someone to run it."

"Then why do you want to buy it?" was Sophie's sensible question.

"I had an idea maybe we could enlarge it. Maybe build a deck out in back with a place to eat."

"Hey, whoa! I live across the street and good Lord, we have enough traffic in Lofton. I vote no. Why don't you start a restaurant near the quarries? Use them as an historical attraction. Lord knows they could use a little jazzing up."

"You might not mind it at all," Gray said. "Just think—you wouldn't have to go in your kitchen all day long. You could go over to the store for lunch every day."

How little we knew each other. I couldn't imagine anything less appealing than going out for lunch every day. Any day, for that matter, except with visiting friends. Gray tried to persuade Sophie to go to the Inn for dinner, but with tears beginning again, she waved wanly and went upstairs.

Gray looked so forlorn I invited him to share a couple of poached eggs on toast with me. I shooed him out the door seconds after he put down his fork.

THIRTEEN

When Detective Butler called early the next morning, Sophie had already gone. She left a note saying that she'd be at Goat Heaven. I was feeding Lulu.

Butler sympathized with me about the rattlesnake episode, but his polite words lacked warmth. In seconds he managed to get my dander up by asking if Sophie liked snakes.

"You can't think Sophie killed Sid Colt and is responsible for Hil's so-called accident? Laid out the dynamite and brought that damn snake into the house?"

"I have to think about what's possible, Mrs. McWhinny. Are there motives? Perhaps Sid Colt was too aggressive about wanting to share the benefits of Hilary Oats's death with your niece. When the victim leaned over, any strong young woman could have delivered the fatal blow. I also think her anger might have been aroused by the dynamite episode, which she could have attributed to the deceased. And possibly the snake and the loosened wheel lugs were Colt's ideas, which your niece felt were ill-advised. Who knows? We must consider all possibilities."

There seemed to be no point in arguing with him, so I asked about Sid. Who, I wanted to know, had been notified of his death?

Butler didn't know any more than Sophie and I knew about Sid. He had talked to the mail-forwarding landlady in Scranton who had shed no light. Sid's uncle's lawyer had died. Butler added that he hoped I'd be home this morning. He planned to come talk to the Millers about Sid and also wanted to talk further to me. We said a chilly goodbye.

After I tidied up the kitchen I strolled around the backyard with Lulu. I waved my arms, taking deep inhalations of the delicious autumn air. I exercised my legs by kicking piles of leaves into the air. I even jogged around my moribund vegetable garden a couple of times. I was reminded by the last bent stalks of dill that I should trot over to the store and buy some vinegar to preserve their appealing flavor.

Refreshed by my romp, I walked around to the front of the house and saw a group gathered in front of the store. The early newspaper crowd was chatting and impatiently checking watches.

The Millers usually opened the store at eight o'clock sharp. My watch said quarter past. I had a fleeting vision of Wanda and Jake cornered in the bedroom by the coiled rattler.

From my side of the street I saw something the newshounds couldn't see. The Millers' faded little Toyota wasn't parked in its usual place behind the town bulletin board.

"Don," I greeted my neighbor, "what's up?"

"Don't know. The Millers don't seem to be bustling around inside. Don't know what's up."

"Their car's gone, so I guess they're not there." I pointed out that the papers were usually left on the side steps of the library.

Don lugged the papers over to the store and distributed them. No one mentioned Sid's murder. The news would come a little later in the local paper.

I didn't register one word I read in yesterday's *Times* while I waited for Detective Butler.

When the phone rang I remembered that I had decided not to call Hilary the night before, but to save all the terrible news for morning. That's who it was—Hilary, sounding mild and patient, maybe a little long-suffering.

"I'll be there before eleven," I promised him, "but first, brace yourself, dear. I have some tragic news." I began with the wet dynamite, which must have raised his blood pressure to dangerous levels. After a description of Sid's murder I could hear him breathing, but neither of us spoke for a bit while I guess he adjusted himself to the horror. "And least, but at least last, there was a rattlesnake in your couch."

"Are you in an altered state? What are you talking about, for Pete's sake? There aren't any rattlers in Lofton."

"Can't talk, Hil. Detective Butler is here. See you soon."

"Sorry to bother you, Mrs. McWhinny," Butler began, "but I can't rouse the Millers. The store seems to be closed."

"Wait a sec," I called. "I have a key.

"Upstairs," I pointed. We entered through the puzzled throng of shoppers on the street. Butler ignored their questions. Too full of apprehension to do more than shrug, I followed Butler up to the Millers' apartment.

The place was empty. The Millers had clearly left in haste. Scattered cardboard boxes partially full made me realize they couldn't fit all their belongings in the car. I wasn't about to poke around. I was too afraid the rattler may have been left behind. I gave the couch a wide berth.

It was a cozy apartment, for which we had supplied a minimum of furniture that included long burlap curtains, the corduroy couch, a dropleaf table and chairs, and a couple of nice old rugs. I'd forgotten that I'd supplied decoration for the walls. One of the paintings made me smile—a portrait of a Berkshire pig I'd painted a million years ago. I remembered its owner rejected the picture as not pretty enough.

Butler came out of the bedroom. "A note, addressed to you."

I unfolded the paper. "We're sorry to leave suddenly. Please tell the others. We have a sick child in Texas."

"Did you know about a child or their children?"

"I don't recall that they were mentioned when we interviewed them."

"And that was how long ago?"

"Oh Lord, I can't remember. I've been on the store committee forever, maybe thirty years or more. Ever since we moved up from New York long ago. But I think we talked with the Millers three or four months ago."

"Have you kept their references?"

I told him we'd have to ask Millie Santini, our librarian, who was the secretary of our group.

Butler was out the door in seconds. The library didn't open until noon. But I thought he deserved to find that out for himself.

With the rattler still in mind, I raced down the stairs after him.

Had the news of Sid's murder made the Millers leave? Or maybe it wasn't news. Maybe Wanda knew that Jake had killed Sid. Or maybe she killed him, though I found it hard to imagine. Wanda couldn't have been feigning shock yesterday. How could Sid have been a threat to either of them?

At home I sat on the porch with Lulu on my lap and wondered if the onset of Alzheimer's disease was a sense of befuddlement. I hoped not. It was the sheer quantity of horrors that confused me. I decided that I'd have to concentrate on a single theme.

Sid Colt was the catalyst as well as the victim. Life in Lofton had been fairly serene until he appeared. Maybe I should talk to the landlady in Scranton, and why wasn't I as equipped as a policeman to find Sid's friend in New York, in the Village that I knew so well? I could get closer to Wyman or anyone else at the quarry who'd talk to me about Sid. The "numero uno" message certainly indicated the lack of a fan club for the deceased.

An hour went by and no Detective Butler. The heck with him. I hadn't promised to sit still all day, but I had promised to call for Hilary before noon.

I left a note for Sophie on the newel post and said goodbye to Lulu and Vanessa, who were arranged in a patch of sunshine on the living room rug.

One of the more trying manifestations of age has to do with single-mindedness, or with the inability to think of more than one thing at a time. With the intention of driving from point A to point B, often I would inadvertently arrive at point C.

I caught myself turning down the road to Manchester when I meant to go in the opposite direction to Brattleboro. So I made myself concentrate on Hilary and how annoyed he'd be if I were late.

Looking pale but rested, Hilary was sitting in a wheelchair in the hospital lobby, swapping war stories with a couple of newfound cronies. One had a three-footed cane and the other leaned on his walker.

"There you are, Tish." He introduced us. "Buddies I didn't meet in the Pacific." He pointed at me. "Meet my keeper."

An orderly saw me and came over to push Hilary through the door, and then helped him into the car.

"I don't need any help, son, but thanks, I guess it's your job." When the orderly had left, Hil turned to me. "Now, Letitia, let's start with the murder. Who did it?"

It seemed incongruous to be describing all the awful events of the last few days against the breathtaking background of the West River winding between its scarlet and crimson banks. We should be tame old leaf-peepers, not people concerned with murder and havoc.

When I ended my recitation by telling Hilary of my plan to investigate Sid's background, he raised a big hand. "Now wait a minute. We're talking about murder, and I don't want to see you, madame, murdered. Let's sit this one out. Let that detective worry about Sid. That's his job, that's how he makes his living. I'm telling you, leave it alone."

"Cool it, commander. The only way to clear Sophie is to find out who is responsible. Sid was the cause of all this. I'm going to find out more about him. Period."

"And I suppose it's futile for me to suggest a good lawyer."

"A lawyer is a fine idea. Why, Hilary, will you tell me, does everyone say a 'good' lawyer? I've never heard anyone say 'What you need is a lawyer.'"

At the stop sign where Route 30 meets Route 11, I audibly drew in my breath at the sight of a small blue car. "That's it. That's the car."

Hilary fell against the door as I wrenched the wheel around. "What the hell are you doing?"

"It may be the car. The one I saw before Sophie's house was

119

blown up. There's something about it. Maybe that bumper sticker. Can you read the thing?"

"Are you kidding?"

Hilary's eyes were worse than mine.

"Maybe I'm crazy. But relax, give in. I'm going to follow it until I figure out why it's so familiar."

Hilary groaned. But short of pulling out the ignition key, there was nothing he could do to stop our chase down Lofty Mountain.

We slowed down when the blue car turned off onto Route 7, the wide highway to Bennington.

"Bennington—we're going to Bennington!" Hilary held his head. "Why didn't I stay in the hospital?"

Near Arlington, Hilary observed that the driver of the blue car knew he was being followed. It was pretty obvious. When the man speeded up, so did I, and when he slowed down so did I.

"I hope he isn't a violent type with a machine gun on the seat beside him," Hil said. "We'd make a great target."

It was a great relief when we both turned off in Bennington. The blue car then made a sharp right beyond the Grand Union and pulled into a parking lot in front of the Universal car rental office.

"This is it, Hil!" I was elated. "See that bumper sticker? It says Universal." We pulled in beside the blue sedan.

The driver jumped out of the car and slammed the door behind him. There was a suggestion of flames coming out of his nostrils as he stormed around to my side of the car. The whites of his eyes made me think of a catalo, the offspring of a steer and a buffalo.

"What the hell do you think you're doing? Are you—" He

paused and addressed his question to Hilary, who, looking like an ancient monarch, had emerged and was standing beside his open door. "Is she crazy?"

I didn't wait for them to come to any manly agreement on that point. Loyal though Hilary was, he had often had reason to doubt my sanity.

I told the man I was sorry and ducked by him into the office.

A tired-looking young woman, chewing on her hair, sat behind a computer. She raised her eyebrows. "Help you?"

"Yes, please. The blue car out there." I pointed out the window. "Do you have that exact same kind of car for rent at all your agencies? You know, in New Hampshire and New York?"

"The Geo? Yup. I'd say it's our major subcompact. You want to rent one?"

Her indifferent manner changed when I asked if she could tell me the names of those who had rented Geos from her and maybe elsewhere, on Tuesday, Wednesday, and Thursday of last week.

"No, ma'am. It's all in here." She pointed at the screen. "And it's confidential."

Her expression when I departed was one of long-suffering resignation.

Thank goodness Hilary, unbloodied, was sitting calmly in the Isuzu. I was relieved to see the sedan's driver had his head and shoulders in the Geo's trunk, so I was able to back out of the lot before he could air more of his thoughts about our tandem drive.

"May I hope we're going home now?"

"You may." I was disappointed that the Universal woman hadn't said, "Yes, an evil-looking man rented a Geo last Thursday," but now I did know that a Geo rented from some Universal place was the car present when Sophie's house was blown up.

"Maybe," I said to Hilary, "maybe I could be hypnotized and come up with something else about the car."

He said he thought the only possibility for me would be self-hypnosis.

I made no response to what I guessed was a sarcastic remark. "You'll be glad to know, Hil, that I'm going to take your suggestion. I'm going to plunk this all in Butler's lap. This kind of thing is right up their alley. These Universal people will have to answer any questions the police ask."

As we entered Lofton, Hilary touched my arm. "I can't take it, Tish. I can't face the idea of going to my house. The idea that someone wanted to kill me makes me sick. Or that someone wanted me to be struck by a rattler—that makes me sick, too. I just don't know how I can go back there yet."

"I wouldn't let you, chum. Vanessa's waiting for you in the library. The yank-out bed in there is seven feet long and, I'm told, comfy."

It made my blood boil to see Hilary so undone. I wanted to point out the rotten person who was responsible for his distress, I wanted to see the murderer convicted, and I wanted Sophie to thumb her nose at Detective Butler.

Hilary slept most of the afternoon, but the chef in him was undaunted, and he cooked a beautiful meal for Sophie and me. He called it a simple supper. He sautéed chanterelles that he gathered in the woods behind my house. We had fresh pasta and a salad of watercress from my brook.

Later, sniffing and sipping Calvados, we talked in circles about the murder, the dynamite, and the snake.

I gave up first, and spent half an hour in the bathtub. Hilary said good night, and Sophie turned in after she walked Lulu.

The house was quiet when I came downstairs to lock the doors and check on Hilary.

"Are you okay, Hil?" I whispered into the darkness.

"No," he replied in an equally soft voice. "But I will be if you get in with me."

His invitation didn't call for much reflection. Chancy to change the playing cards, but I figured we could both use a little forgetfulness. I got in.

FOURTEEN

I slept later than usual, and instead of shuffling downstairs in my bathrobe and slippers I got dressed before breakfast.

Deep thought and decision-making were not part of the process. An armoire in the hall contained what I considered my real clothes—suits, long skirts and dressy tops, plus an assortment of dresses, a long black velvet cape, and what I called New York shoes. My daily wardrobe consisted of a vast collection of garments that Sophie called period preppie. There were at least a dozen of Doug's old button-down shirts, soft as hankies. Endless slacks, from ancient flannel to medium-chic corduroy and tweed, and stacks of jeans. The shoe department was where I lost my grip. I'll spare you a description of my multicolored sneakers or the long shelf of mistakes I can't seem to part with. Doug's huge mahogany chiffonier held my rainbow collection of turtlenecks from L.L. Bean to Saks Fifth Avenue.

The turtleneck group was growing because I was under the impression that they hid my aging, wrinkled neck. However, I've noticed in snapshots of myself that the collars appear to be holding up my head like a scoop of ice cream in a cup.

Sophie looked surprisingly well. "How did you sleep, dear?"

"Like a log and all night long, thank heavens."

"And you, Hilary?"

"Like a baby. That's a comfortable bed in the library."

"Good. I haven't had any complaints."

"I'll bet you haven't." Hilary smiled and handed me *The New York Times*. "Read all about it—second section, page thirty-two."

Sophie brought me coffee as I read the brief report. The absent homeowner, Hilary Oats, was described as a retired publisher and longtime member of the community, and the honorary chief of the volunteer fire department. I was an artist and widow who lived nearby. Sophie was a young glamorous breeder of goats. The police, the *Times* reported, had no leads at the moment. Sid's murder was the single topic; there was no mention of dynamite, loose lugs, rattlers, or Sophie's nuked house.

"You've been to the store, Hil. What's going on over there?"

"It's a madhouse, but fret not. Hilda and Joe are pinch-hitting. They asked me to tell you not to worry, they'll stick around. The natives are restive and the press is beginning to appear. Unless you want to bare your soul or have your picture in the paper, I'd suggest you keep the doors locked."

"Let's see." I walked to the front of the house. From one of the living room windows I could see what Hilary meant. Where usually three or four cars and pickups might be parked by the store, there were a dozen or more. Friends were talking in groups and people came in and out of the store. There were enough dogs milling around to start a pound.

I ducked back when I saw the glint of a camera lens and

thought of all the news photographs I'd seen of someone furtively or shyly peering from behind a parted curtain.

"I used your phone, Tish, to call Ruth." Hil was getting into his jacket. "She's probably at the house by now so I'm leaving. Can Vanessa stay here today? Sophie's convinced the viper had a mate and if that snake ever even winked at a female of the species Ruth'll find her, it, whatever. I'll call you at noon. See what you have on your devious mind. Maybe I can be of help. And, need I say, thank you."

To see Hil striding up the road, you'd never believe he'd been pulled out of a ditch just three days ago.

Millie Santini came trotting toward the house from the other direction. Her mop of gray hair was frizzier than mine. In the sunshine it formed a beach-ball-sized halo around her head. Wire-rimmed round glasses framed her lively dark eyes. "Phew! What is it, just quarter of nine and I'm exhausted already. Hilary told you about Hilda and Joe. Thank God for little and big favors. They're wonderful and, for the moment at least, they're both having fun."

I told Millie about Graham Gray's wish to buy the store and his ideas for an addition.

"A deli with tables? Spare us! Let's have a meeting next week. He can make a proposal. Who is this guy, I mean, what's he like? I've seen him in the store. Tall and skinny, right?"

"Gray. Graham Gray. He's likable, polite, and considerate. Oh, I don't know . . . "

"Don't think he's going to blow me away—but does he sound like a storekeeper? I mean, what goes on in his head?"

"You've got me, Millie. Ask Sophie; she knows him better."

"That I can believe. Is Sophie all right? Poor kid. Just had an idea. If we had storekeepers who lived elsewhere, like Hilda and

Joe, we could rent the upstairs apartment and make enough to pay the taxes, and so on."

Of course Sophie came to mind. But this was not the time for domestic action. I had Greenwich Village on my mind.

A little later I was lucky to find my friend Kay in her office when I called New York. She said I was welcome to use her flat, that she was leaving for Milan tomorrow afternoon. I cherished the key to her tiny Bleecker Street apartment and I hoped her peripatetic job as a fashion reporter would last indefinitely.

In a way I was glad I couldn't rush off to the City that very moment. It would give me the afternoon to concentrate on Edgar Wyman, his wife, or anyone else at Ethan Allen who would talk to me.

Before I'd finished cleaning up in the kitchen, Gray appeared and brought news that the police had found Sid's car at Pete's garage. He'd left it there two days ago, and Gray guessed he had gone right from Pete's to Hilary's house.

We were standing on the porch when we saw Butler coming out of the store. He spotted us and wove his way through the reporters and dogs to join us.

Gray asked him if Sid had left a will.

Butler said no such document had surfaced, but they had been in contact with the new owners of the quarry, who told him that the four million paid for the quarry had been made out to the Alpha Company and, as Gray had told me, had been deposited in a bank in Nassau. Butler said the bank refused to divulge any information about Alpha Company, for the moment a dead end.

The whole business sounded very fishy to me. All the more reason to delve into Sid's background.

It's hard to believe that Butler was reading my mind when he said that a background search on Sid had revealed nothing of importance, and until they found the Millers, there was no other source of information.

When Butler left, Gray said he didn't think much of the detective. "He doesn't act as though he's really trying. Know what I mean?"

I did. And thought about the man as I polished off the household chores. In spite of his revelations to me the day before yesterday, his attitude didn't inspire trust or invite confidences. Sophie described him as having the social graces of a dead anchovy. He actually yawned when I told him about the Universal Rental Company using Geos. He perked up just slightly when I told him Gray's desire to buy the store. "You could use someplace to eat around here." He'd nodded his approval to Gray. "Good idea."

Would Butler let Sophie be a scapegoat just because of his unfortunate mind-set or a lack of attention or energy? Not if I could help it.

Sweet as he was, I could even suspect Gray, a thought that clearly hadn't occurred to Butler. I mean, why buy the store if he didn't want to run it? Lord knows the place couldn't be described as an exciting financial investment. Maybe Gray fantasized that his actions would improve his image with Sophie, and he, like Sid, would probably love to win Sophie as well as be Lord of the manor. But murder Sid? I had to admit it seemed unlikely.

Since my house appeared to have become an official meeting place the last few days, I'd been neglecting Lulu. So I laced up a pair of dizzy new sneakers and took her out by the back door.

Someone had expounded in a newspaper article that dirt roads were considered very toney by well-heeled country buffs.

The author sneered at such affectation as a pathetic attempt to play the part of a rustic sophisticate.

A pox on all that nonsense. Dirt roads are beautiful; who needs another reason? Show me the shadows on a tar road that can compare with the lavender, ochre, or melon gray of a dirt road. The town had sent Turk Smith to road-scraping school last year, and as much as I disliked the boor, it was a treat to see him handle our road-grading dinosaur. Our roads were perfection.

We walked past half a dozen houses tucked in the woods or perched on a hill, and I wondered what life would be like away from bustling downtown Lofton. Even though there were only six establishments on Main Street—our store, the post office, the antique barn, the church, the Inn, and Pete's garage—I knew I'd miss every one of them. On the way home I saw that the crowd at the store had diminished, so I stopped in to say hello to the Littles.

"Tish." Big Hilda enveloped me in a huge hug. Her bosom was like a Victorian bed bolster, and only a quick turn of my head saved me from suffocation.

I'd been on the receiving end of Hilda's hugs before, and because of her height she tended to lean back, lifting her bosom buddies off the floor.

When she put me down, she picked up Lulu and gave her a noisy kiss on her stop, that downy dent between her eyes and her pug nose.

Joe, who was waiting on a group of campers from nearby Hapgood Pond, was less effusive but equally warm.

"The old lady's in her element as Madame Storekeeper," said the retired New Jersey banker, who could have passed as the typical country store proprietor, whatever that is.

Hilda asked if I'd seen the *Bennington Banner,* and handed it to me folded to show a two-paragraph item underlined and circled.

The gist of it was that a paper bag with a timber rattler in it had been found in front of the museum the previous morning. A skull and crossbones done with a red marker cautioned the finder and asked that the rattler be cared for.

"The Millers," Hilda said. "Right?"

"How did you know about the snake?"

"Ruth. She just stopped in on her way home from Hilary's."

Joe handed us each a sliver of country cheddar. "What's happening here, Tish? It's unbelievable. Dynamite, murder, rattlesnakes. In books, yes. But in Lofton? Heaven help us."

There was nothing to be learned by staying in town, so I called Hilary to see if he was game for a trip to Ethan Allen.

He was, and said that in spite of what Hil called Ruth's ruthless ways, she hadn't expelled the aura of evil from his house.

"The word is hate, Tish. I still feel sick to think anyone hates me so much and hates Sophie, for that matter. After all, she might have been home that day. I feel naked and vulnerable. Sure I'll join you."

Hate wasn't the word, I thought. Greed or lust for power was more like it. Someone wanted something, and Sophie, Hilary, and poor Sid were just in the way. Unimportant as human beings, they were obstacles to be frightened off or eliminated.

Thinking rattler, I put on field boots. I knew when I pulled out a stout walking stick that it was silly. Did I think a rattler was going to sit still while I hit it? Carrying on with reptilian thoughts, I took some winter gloves out of the hall drawer and dragged out a tattered old hip-length leather coat of Doug's.

Hilary had a flair for costumes. His belted sports jackets were from Savile Row in the thirties. His knickerbockers were chic before his time; maybe they were inherited from his father. Argyle socks were Hil's passion, and his skiff-sized loafers usually sported tassels.

He appeared today in the guise of a hunter, with suede patches at the elbows and shoulders of his jacket, vintage riding breeches, and—in spite of his denial of herpetophobia—handsome leather puttees. Binoculars hung around his neck and a pipe, upside down, was clenched between his teeth.

"Where's your gun?"

"How insulting. I rely on superior intellect and eloquent delivery. Where's your brush hook and your bundle of fagots?"

What a pair of old dragons!

Enthroned in the Trooper and aimed north, I could feel Hilary looking at me.

"Well," I said, "you must be admiring my profile."

We all know that people grow to look like their dogs. I was no exception.

"I know what you're thinking, Tish. You're thinking, 'Is that old goat so pleased with himself that he's going to be a pain in the neck?' "

You can't fool old friends. That's exactly what I had been thinking: the cost of altering our relationship. Should I have said good night and padded back upstairs instead of staying to have a surprisingly lovely time?

Hilary's emotional deep-freeze since his wife's death was a condition I thought was permanent. That, or maybe he was convinced he couldn't perform and had accepted it as a fact of life. In either case, last night in the library must have been a revelation for him. It certainly had been for me.

"Nothing's changed, Tish. Except I feel about twenty years

younger. I hereby empower you to say 'buzz off' any time you feel I'm breathing down your neck."

"Last night was nice, Hil. I mean, really nice, but let's not analyze it, shall we? I do think that the yank-out bed is a little small for four."

"Four?"

"You didn't notice that Vanessa and Lulu joined us?"

"Can't say as I did. But I hear you, Tish. I gather the topic's not up for discussion. Right?"

"Right."

FIFTEEN

Slate was discovered in Vermont and in New York State in about 1843. Then the influx began.

Miners from Wales surged into the area, followed by workers from Poland, Italy, and Hungary. In the heyday of the industry, from the turn of the century until the depressed thirties, there were more than fifty quarries in operation. Today there are less than half that number. Many of the present miners are descendants of the original workers. Even so, it is becoming very difficult for the quarries to find young men willing to do such back-breaking work. They'd rather sit in front of a computer and take home better pay. Or so concluded Hilary, who had been reading a history of Vermont because the nurse had parked his wheelchair in the hospital library for much of his sojourn.

"And, as you know," Hilary said, "the prospering railroads and the interest of New York bankers opened the industry to its global possibilities."

"Did you know there are slate tombs as far back as five hundred B.C.?" I said, and added, "Maybe even earlier."

"I like to think little Neanderthal families built slate patios outside their caves," Hilary said. "You know, for cookouts."

I wondered aloud if there was intense competition between the quarries all operating in such close proximity. Hilary said that Wyman had told him on our last visit that it wasn't a problem, as most of the quarries produced different slate products. He also said that there were quite a few families that mined in their own backyards and could then sell their rock to the larger companies.

"What, may I ask, is the object of this trip, Tish? I discount idle tourism."

Earlier I had called Elvira Wyman, I explained, and told her I'd be sketching at the pit and hoped she could join me. I hated to think I was going to pump the nice woman again—worse yet, trap her into revealing something of her husband's activities. Gregarious Hilary, I told him, was supposed to chat up anyone he could nab to quiz them about Sid and, if possible, about Edgar Wyman.

Hilary took off when I spotted Elvira. This time she was wearing a long beaked fisherman's cap. White letters on dark blue spelled KENNEBUNK, MAINE.

"Now that's a great eyeshade."

She took it off. "For you. I have another one at home. It's Edgar's and he won't wear it."

I demurred but accepted the gift with genuine pleasure. My eyes relaxed under the long visor.

We both chose a line of open sheds for our subject matter. Elvira explained that the huge chunks of slate being sheltered needed to be kept warm during the impending winter. I remembered what Phil had told me but refrained from saying, "Yes, I know."

"Are you and your husband old Vermonters?"

"Oh, sure. Edgar's great-grandfather worked in this very pit. Me, I'm a Vermonter, too, but the first generation in my family to be born here. My parents came from Italy—Trento. My father worked in Boston. He took care of the garden at Mrs. Jack Gardner's museum."

"That devastating robbery! I wish they'd find the paintings. Was your father there then?"

Elvira said he had died, and in response to my questions said she had six brothers, one in Vermont and the others scattered around New England. "The brother who gave us the caps, he was here last week for a family do. He has a cold storage plant in Kennebunk."

"I have to go to Maine soon," I said. "How long does it take them to drive over?"

"Oh, Lord, forever. It's one of those you-can't-get-there-from-here trips. They'd never make it in their smelly pickup. They rent."

I hoped I didn't look as wide-eyed as I felt.

"I love to rent cars," I said fatuously. "Gives you a chance to see what's new in the market. Last time I rented one it was a Honda—no, it was a Geo. That's what it was. Cute."

"Theirs was a Geo, a blue Geo." Elvira turned slowly, comprehension dulling her eyes. Disgust and revulsion turned her face gray. "A Geo. So that's what all this let's-be-pals-and-paint-together is all about. Let's have a picnic. You stink, Mrs. McWhinny!" She threw her chalk box and pad through her car window and ran to the other side. "Do you know that, lady? You stink!"

Tears clouded her eyes as she fiercely wheeled her car in a circle and gunned it, leaving me in a shower of slate dust.

135

Elvira was right. I was a stinker, a tawdry conniving skunk. I could have stood her anger, but her tears, no. I was mortally ashamed of myself. What could I make of Elvira's brother's rented Geo? Did he lend the car to Wyman? This time I was determined to dump my Geo findings forcefully in Butler's lap, goad him, pester him, insist, if I could, that he investigate the matter. I couldn't look Elvira in the eye again.

I quit any pretense of sketching and skulked around in a manner befitting my mood. The whine of saws came from the sheds on either side of where I was parked, but no one was in sight. I'd had an idea the other night in bed and walked over to the blackboard shed, the place where numero uno had been described. I had hoped to find the young worker, but no one was there, either. Neither was there a numero uno message on any of the stacked blackboards.

Remembering the idea momentarily raised me out of the slough. It was about a blackboard telephone table. A slate of some shape on proper legs with an old-fashioned school eraser attached. Jot down a number or a message with a piece of chalk and be able to erase it. My imagination raced. I was practically in business. Sophie could augment her income and run the place. The design over my garage door could read: A CLEAN SLATE. Maybe that was too square. We'd get Hil involved. He was good at coining names.

I peered into the working sheds. No Hilary. I wondered who he had pinned to what wall to answer his questions.

There were other small slate pits being worked by Ethan Allen, all out of sight, but Sid had described them as just a yell away. Maybe Hilary had found it easier to collar Wyman or one of the miners there than at the forbidding main pit.

From what Wanda had said, I felt sure no sensible rattler

would be hanging out on a zippy fall day like today. But the hot sun made me cautious and I felt happier back in the Trooper.

It was hard to get Elvira's face out of my mind. I put my forehead against my arms folded on the wheel.

Of course Wyman must have been interrogated by Butler. The suspicion or almost certainty that Wyman could lose his job must have been devastating. And more than his job, to lose his sense of importance; the miners called him "boss"—a powerful word. Even though I felt terribly sorry for his wife, I couldn't help suspecting that Wyman's tortured mind thought the only way he could bring a mountain of bad cess down on Sid was by blowing up Sophie's house with company dynamite. I had no way of knowing if Butler had quizzed him further after I told him about my trip to Universal Car Rental. But Elvira's reaction made me sure that he had.

Where was the boss? Where was Hilary?

In low gear I crept around the rim of the pit with no sign of either man. Even if Hilary was down with the comma-sized men in the bottom of the quarry, I knew I'd have recognized his erect stature and thick white hair.

Still in first gear, I drove up the road toward the minor pits. Twice I cringed as monster trucks surged by, and just as I was about to turn into what seemed to be a quarry road I was startled by mad honking behind me and a car rushing by. I thought it might have grazed me. Coming to a stop at the edge of a pit, the men jumped out of their cars and ran out of sight.

Not pausing to examine the side of my car, I tore after the men on foot. I could tell the breathlessness of an emergency when I saw it.

The men had vanished. I literally skidded to a stop at the rim of the pit and looked straight down what I guessed to be about six stories into a jagged hole. The pit wasn't as symmetrical as the big quarry. Rock jutted into the opening like the prow of a battleship and an eyebrow of overhanging rock made the far side of the pit look grim and dangerous.

People were moving below, but with my lousy eyes I couldn't sort out the action. I didn't see Hilary. I jogged as fast as I dared down a path suitable for bulldozers, praying that I wouldn't turn an ankle on the treacherous mix of rock and gravel.

I nearly jumped into the next world when a deafening honk blasted out behind me. The minivan would have run over me if I hadn't jumped.

"Oh, shit-shit-shit." With sharp rocks digging into my bottom I hugged my knee to my chest. The red-hot pain was fierce.

I kept repeating my shit mantra spiced with other comments about the van driver. What heedless cretin would try to run over a gray-haired woman on the brink of a canyon?

Getting out of bed with one nonfunctional leg is tough, but try getting over and up on a pile of rocks with death beckoning from below. It's not possible. I huddled there, moaning and cursing. Yelling wouldn't have helped. The sounds from below were far away, muted and unintelligible.

Piecing things together later, I thought I must have been there for ten minutes before the minivan reappeared. This time it was crawling up the steep grade and, thank God, stopped beside me. Men walking behind the van ran to my side.

"Edgar Wyman, oh thank goodness. Help, it's my damn knee."

Maybe the workers were used to picking up fallen comrades, because they were surprisingly deft and gentle. One of them opened the back of the van and the others slid me inside.

"What the hell." Hilary was propped up in the back seat of

the van. His arm was in a rope sling and, with a bloody bandana tied around his head, he looked like a drop-out from the Minute Men parade. "What happened to you?" My reply was laced with angry four-letter words.

"I hear you, lady," the driver said. "Sure am sorry, but it was an emergency."

"You're the emergency, Hil. What happened to you?"

Hilary said he had walked around to see if he could find Wyman at one of the smaller pits. He saw a pickup and assumed it belonged to Wyman and that he might be down below. He stood by the edge of the pit and was scanning the scene with his binoculars when something bumped him from behind and sent him crashing over the edge and down.

"I don't know why you're not dead!"

"I may be, I'm not sure. If I'd fallen the whole way it would have been curtains. I rolled about fifteen or twenty feet of sheer hell till my coat caught on an outcropping. Then I wormed my way down. I couldn't go up or sideways, I had to go down. Slid again the last ten feet or so. They think I broke my arm and cut my head, but there's no part of me that doesn't hurt. I think both legs are broken.

"One thing, Tish, you don't have to expect any old lothario to be breathing down your neck. I think I broke the thing off."

Hilary hadn't lost his sense of humor, but we both nearly did, sitting in wheelchairs in the Rutland hospital emergency room. We had to wait, we were told, because a bus accident had all the hospital staff busy. At least it was encouraging to know they didn't think me terminal.

Wyman came in to say my car was outside. He'd driven it over from the quarry, and he said he had also called Sophie, who was on her way to drive us home when we were released.

I tugged at Wyman's sleeve. "Do me a favor, please. In the glove compartment of the Trooper you'll find a leather-covered flask. Please get it for us."

He looked doubtful but returned in minutes. After looking furtively around the waiting room, he put it in my lap.

Hilary and I, without a word, turned our wheelchairs' backs to the entry desk and took long swigs of bourbon. Too bad to use whiskey as medicine, but it felt awfully good going down.

"How did you happen to find me?" Hilary asked Wyman, who was chewing his lower lip.

"One of the boys said he'd seen someone walk up the road to number three. I looked around and then spotted you below. I was sure you'd be dead. That's a fifty-foot drop. You gotta be made of steel."

"Rubber." Hilary displayed the gory palms of his hands. "I inched down most of it. Then what?"

"You heard me, or maybe you were sort of out of it. I called on my walkie and the boys came. Then the first-aid team."

"I didn't see your pickup when I drove in," I said.

"Didn't have it. I was on foot."

"It felt like a car bumper, or something really hard that hit me on the back side." Hilary groaned. "I *think* I saw the pickup when I walked over to the edge of the pit. Yes, I'm sure I did."

"I didn't see it," Wyman said. "I never take the keys out. We all use it around here. Like the trucks, it doesn't even have license plates. The whole fleet just operates on quarry property."

Dr. Broadbent affirmed the diagnosis that was made at the quarry by Hilary's rescuers, but in more precise terms. A cracked ulna and a laceration on the frontal area of his skull. Those, and multiple bruises. Miraculously, my patella wasn't crushed, my ligaments were untorn, and what I had was a major bruise. A description that sounded too mild to cause such fierce pain.

Sophie dashed in just as the doctor was delivering parting instructions and was about to parcel out medication. I was touched by her concern as she cooed over us. She stopped just short of scolding us for being so foolish.

Dr. Broadbent addressed Sophie. "Your grandfather should take no more than three of these in twenty-four hours." He handed her an envelope of pills. "And Grandma can take these for pain when needed but not to be taken with—"

"Excuse me, Doctor," Hilary said. "Mrs. McWhinny and I are both natives of America. We both speak the language, and neither of us is demented. What's more, we're not this young lady's grandparents."

"Oh well," the doctor said, still speaking to Sophie, "the directions are on the packets."

"Oh, good," Hil said. "We can read, too."

Sophie wisely pulled me up, got a grip on Hil's good arm, and propelled us out the door.

Hilary's vim faded when we got into the car, a tortuous process for both of us. The only thing he said during the trip home was, "Please pass the flask." His head fell on his chest and his long arms were folded around his ribs. For once, I didn't recommend that Sophie consider obeying the speed limits.

SIXTEEN

Before I went to bed I dragged out a slim but capacious suitcase to enforce my determination to go to New York the next day.

Lulu let me sleep in the morning until eight o'clock; then she raced off to see if there was any action in the kitchen. I was reluctant to roll the old body out of bed. Black and blue are colors I love in a scarf or dress but I didn't look forward to seeing my mottled hide.

A shampoo was the first order of the day, a deed accomplished in the shower, a long hot shower that undid a few kinks and soothed my knee. My bottom was lavender; the darker tones would come later.

I sat on my chaise longue to tend my knee. Using most of the salve the doctor had given me, I wrapped the sorry-looking joint in soft old Ace bandages and pulled on black tights to hold my handiwork in place.

Next, my gray flannel skirt went on over my head and I chose a red cotton turtleneck for courage and a suede vest for warmth.

After a slow trip downstairs I made my way to the umbrella stand by the front door. Voices from the kitchen sounded like a talk show in progress.

Doug and I both fancied walking sticks and I had a large collection to choose from. I picked out a handsome carved number a godchild had brought me from Jakarta. Then, undecided, I pulled out a hefty stick, a shepherd's cane that we had bought in Montana. It occurred to me it might make a better weapon.

"Who are you going to clobber, Tish?" The question was from Sophie, who found me holding a stick in each hand.

"Are you kidding? I couldn't fight off a sparrow today, but I like this shepherd's hook. It feels good. How's Hilary?"

"Pretty good. You know Hil, he's nuts. Here he nearly gets killed a couple of times and he still thinks yesterday may have been an accident. He just can't believe anyone would want to hurt him. But good Lord, neither can I."

"Who else is in the kitchen?"

"Just Gray. I met him getting the paper. For what it's worth, he thinks Butler is impossible. Says Hilary should hire a private investigator. Maybe he's right. What do you think?"

"First I'd like to follow the only lead we have to Sid's immediate past, that George person. I wish you could bring up some added insight about him. It's pretty slim pickings. I mean, what do we know? One: he's really involved in yoga. Two: his name is George something. Three: he's someplace in Greenwich Village. Not much."

"Not enough to send an invalid out looking for him. You can't go hobbling around the city with that knee, Tish. You and Hil are both nuts."

Sophie put her hand to her mouth. "Something Sid said—

143

'nuts'—made me think of it. I said to Sid, like maybe George had gone back to India, and Sid sort of laughed and allowed as how George would be right there in the Village. 'He wasn't that nuts.' And, oh—Sid said George took a lot of the pictures we saw of India."

"Owns a camera. What a stunning clue."

"Listen, I'm trying."

"Sorry, dear." I patted her hand. An annoying old-folks gesture I must stop doing. "Will you look after Hil if I do go?"

"Well, sure. But Hil's already talked to Ruth. Most of her summer people have gone. She's going to call for him any minute now."

Gray came into the living room with Vanessa held around his neck like a hunter's four-legged victim. The cat was in heaven but far from dead. She was purring like an idling automobile. I reached up and plucked a tiny bouquet of Vanessa's hair from Gray's collar. "You'll be sorry, my friend."

Before I had a chance to see Hilary, Detective Butler knocked on the door.

We greeted him with varying degrees of warmth. Hilary couldn't see him from the kitchen but called out a hello. Sophie, sober-faced, said good morning, and Gray nodded and said "Morning, officer." I lied and said "Glad to see you," but maybe I wasn't lying because I was anxious to know if he'd proceeded on all the information I'd given him on the phone yesterday afternoon. It made me wince to think of it, but I'd even told him how Elvira Wyman described me.

Butler made it clear that he wanted to speak to Hilary and me, so Sophie and Gray tactfully departed for the barn, and the detective and I joined Hilary in the kitchen.

In spite of an all-encompassing sling on his arm, Hilary was brewing a fresh pot of coffee. He groaned as he bent over and put his bandaged head in the oven.

"Perfect timing. The biscuits are done." Hil made baking powder biscuits using half whole-wheat flour. Delicious.

We passed the honey and my favorite kumquat marmalade. We sipped and munched until Butler prodded us for more details of our horrible day at the quarry.

"There's just so much I can tell you about being hit by something I didn't see." Hil poured more coffee. "And as you may imagine, I'd like to think it was an accident."

Butler and I looked at each other. He frowned, and I said, "I'd like to think so, too, but can't."

"About the Wymans"—Butler folded his arms—"I've talked to them. While we have no proof whatsoever, it is possible that Edgar Wyman could have used his brother-in-law's rented car while the rest of the family visited yet another brother in Saratoga. They used Mrs. Wyman's car. Mrs. Wyman's brother agrees that Edgar Wyman could have taken his car, and since they were not charged for mileage by Universal, the brother said he never looked at the indicator."

"You mean the man could have blown up Sophie's house?" Hilary said.

"That is correct."

"So what we have is conjecture. No proof."

"That is correct. Unless, of course, Mrs. McWhinny could identify the car or the plates, it is conjecture. No proof."

Hilary asked if anyone had come forward to claim Sid's remains.

Butler shook his head. "No. Like I told Mrs. McWhinny, we can't locate any family through his Ethan Allen connections or in Scranton where he came from."

"Did he have a passport?"

"Yes, expired. With a brother's name as next of kin. Lewis Colt. He left Scranton four or five years ago. The authorities down there said he was a generation older than Sid and a World War Two veteran with health problems. They guessed he might even have died."

"He's probably dead," Hilary said. "Or his uncle's lawyer would have found him before Sid inherited the quarry. So what do you do now?"

"Wait a little. We placed an obit in the Scranton paper." He shrugged. "We'll see."

"Do you really think Wyman tried to kill me at the quarry? And if so, why?"

"Dunno. I wish I could say there was some hard evidence to work with."

"I hope you've removed Sophie as a suspect?" I said.

"I don't know, ma'am. Who else is there?"

"The Millers. How about either of them? I take it you still haven't found them. Why did they rush off in the night?"

"You told me they'd been thinking about leaving Lofton."

"Sure. But not like that. I can't help thinking that Sid's his own clue. We've got to find out more about him."

"We're doing all we can. It's hopeless to look for someone in New York City when all you know is a first name. No address, no physical description, no nothing." Butler shrugged again and took a last slurp of coffee.

Those damn dark glasses. I wish I could see what the man was thinking.

"Detective Butler, may I ask if you always wear those dark glasses? Doesn't it make the world awfully black on a day like today?"

"Always, ma'am. I'm used to the dark. I'm an albino, can't take the light." He ran his fingers over his straight mousy hair. "I dye my hair, or at least my wife does. She said I just look like a pair of glasses walking around when my hair is natural, sort of like flax."

At some point I guess we all ask an intrusive question like that and, like me, wince with embarrassment for having done so.

"I think he looks like a movie star," a smiling Hilary filled the breech. "So, I ask again, do we just wait?"

"The government is still very interested in finding the dynamite that wasn't used to blow up Miss Beaumont's house or in the box planted at your house. They figure there's another box—somewhere."

"Where are they looking?"

"Who knows? You'll have to ask Agent Rawby. We cooperate just fine but we don't read over each other's shoulder. Tell you one thing. You may not like this, Mr. Oats, but since you seem to be an endangered species, we're going to put a couple of our retired boys on the job. They'll take turns looking out for you."

"That's silly, a waste of time. Ruth, my housekeeper, is going to stay with me. She can handle anything or anybody."

"Sorry, it's all set. The boys won't bother you, but you'll see them around. You can always let out a yell. Think it would make you feel better."

"It makes *me* feel better, especially since I'm going to New York this afternoon."

"New York?" Both men looked at me with raised eyebrows. At least Butler was probably raising his behind those big shades.

"With that watermelon knee, Tish, you crazy? Why don't you wait till I'm better and we'll both go?"

147

l get carried away with embroidery when I'm lying and I think I managed to convince them both that a haircut and a lust for some new shoes provided acceptable female motivation.

After admonishing me to stay out of trouble, Butler drove off. He left me with the feeling that my insensitive question about his dark glasses had eased our relationship. Maybe the feeling was all on my part. His difficult distinction made him seem more human, more likable to me.

Hilary sat on the arm of the couch cradling his bad arm. He looked glum. Why, he wanted to know, would I go to New York without him?

"There's nothing I can do here and I certainly can't concentrate on work. You've heard, and so have I, that if a murder isn't solved in the first week it probably never will be. I want answers. I want to clear Sophie of any suspicion and I want to find out who the maniac is who is trying to kill you."

I picked up Hil's free hand. "Look at this paw of yours. You couldn't even hold a teaspoon, much less flag a taxi. You can't come to New York."

"I know that, but why the hell do you have to go right now when you know it's futile and you may wreck your knee for life? And anyhow, why chase this vague George? The obvious suspects are the Millers. I mean, where are they? What do murderers do? They flee. They don't want to get caught. I know you're looking cross-eyed at Gray, too; but look again, here he is wiggling around underfoot like a spaniel wanting to be patted. Don't go."

Gray wasn't on my mind at the moment. It was George. I knew he'd be in the Village, and even if I didn't find him, the truth is that as much as I wanted to defend my loved ones in Vermont (and I wasn't doing a very good job), I wanted, too, to get away for a day or two. I wasn't used to being surrounded. E.B. White once wrote something to the effect that New York could bestow the gift of privacy. I could hardly wait!

Hilary and Sophie had made it clear they thought my trip was insane—and worse, stupid. But I was convinced that someone called George, who lived in Greenwich Village, would instantly become a Villager. I couldn't imagine him joining a yoga group on 93rd Street or 125th Street, nor in Queens, the Bronx, or Staten Island. Yoga on Staten Island? Come on. How many yoga establishments or gurus could there be in the Village? I'd find out.

"I'm going. Fini, pau, kaput, that's it. Au revoir, arrividerci, adios, so long."

"Stubborn old bitch."

I rubbed the back of his neck. "Your poor old head, battered twice in three—or is it four—days? It's bone-mending time. Please let Ruth pamper you and promise me you'll take it easy. Slow and easy."

"As an old sailor, I'm a little suspicious of evil events coming in threes. Don't worry, I won't do anything cute."

Hilary smoothed down his hair where I'd mussed it. The first bump was a lot worse than yesterday's. "If that man driving behind me had reported my accident sooner I think my head would have benefited by earlier treatment."

"The man behind you! This is the first I've heard about him. Tell me."

"Nothing to tell. I look forward, not behind, when I drive. Just know there was a car on my tail."

"What did he look like?"

"Look like? How would I know? He/she/child—black or white—all the same to me."

"The car?"

"Just a car. Maybe a dark color."

"Have you told Butler?"

"No, forgot about it till now. Don't see how it will help."

"Tell him anyhow."

"Yes, boss; sure, boss."

"Don't be like that, Hilary. Think. If whoever was following you was the same person who loosened your lugs, he may think you can identify him. So he wants you out of the way. Permanently."

"So. Enough of that. I said I'd tell him."

I think Hilary was a little miffed that I didn't urge him to go with me. But I'd never be able to sneak around accompanied by Hil. Thanks to his height, ruddy complexion, and wavy white hair, people glanced at him and appeared to be mildly perplexed, as though Hilary was an old actor whose name they should know, whereas I wanted to operate like an old gray tabby looking for a mouse.

We heard Ruth before we saw her. She had no use for the gradual approach to anything—an example of which was the abrupt way she applied the brakes on her rusty old Cadillac.

Ruth yoo-hooed and ascended the four steps to my porch in two. Huge boots on her skinny legs and an XL lumber shirt made me think of Popeye's bride, Olive Oyl.

"Ta-da." She smote her chest. "Hiya, Tish. Where's the old fart?"

"Oh Ruth, you're impossible. Didn't your mother ever wash your mouth out with soap when you were little?"

"My mother? Hell, I hardly ever saw her, and my grandma swears worse than I do."

Hilary delighted in Ruth's raunchy vocabulary, but I noticed he was less than charmed when I let loose with a stream of my favorite expletives, and he looked offended when Sophie used her selection of four-letter words.

Ruth had the loudest laugh in Lofton. When she threw back her head, opened her quarry-sized mouth and bleated, the sound echoed all over Clement Hollow.

Measured by most yardsticks, Ruth didn't have much to laugh about. A drunken father, an absent mother, and the slightest allowable education did nothing to squash her zest for life or her reputation for earthy wisdom. She could be forty or sixty or Hil's age, it didn't matter. All the wrinkles in her face went in the right direction.

"Well, look at you, Gramps. Bet you pushed him over the edge, Tish. Will you ever look at what they done to a plain old sling these days? Looks like a truss. Good thing I'm gonna take care of you." Ruth put her arm around Hilary's waist and guided him down the steps.

Hil smiled tenderly at his pint-sized friend. "If Detective Butler had met you, Ruth, he'd call off those ex-cops he's assigned to protect me."

"Oh, I know all those guys." She laughed. "Maybe we can get up a game of poker."

Lucky Hilary, I thought, to have a dragon lady friend like Ruth who'd lay down her life for him as would he for her.

"Whoops!" Ruth, already in the car, pushed open the mammoth door and jumped out. She leaped up the porch steps. "Forgot something." She darted into the house to return with Vanessa under her arm. "Almost forgot Mrs. Oats."

SEVENTEEN

Innocuous clothes for the Village were easy to find. Gray or black slacks, a trench coat, and, of course, comfortable shoes. Uptown clothes were different, but I didn't expect to stray above Fourteenth Street, my mental image of the sartorial boundary. Not that it mattered anymore. When Hilary and I went to see Tosca at the Met last April, we were disheartened by the sight of so many people wearing blue jeans and shirtsleeves. Bye-bye old-fashioned dress codes. I'm glad we've been emancipated in the clothing department, but at the opera, well, I miss the gala look.

I also got out a voluminous shoulder bag, and aside from the basics (minimal make-up, a wallet, keys, and Kleenex), I packed a very small camera and a hand-sized spray can of picture varnish, my version of mace. I included my Swiss army knife, which was indispensable not only in the boudoir, the kitchen, and on the workbench, but a versatile tool that, on one desperate occasion, I almost used to perform a tracheotomy on a guy I barely knew. I always carried a sketch pad and a clatter of pens.

If it had been my right knee that connected with the pile of slate, I couldn't have driven the car to Albany.

We Loftonites regard the railroad parking lot in Albany a wonderfully safe place to leave a car for a trip to the city. It appears that the legislators frown on car thieves, so demand and get twenty-four-hour surveillance for all cars parked at the station.

A train gliding in from Chicago stopped just long enough for a kind conductor to help me aboard. Inside, another Samaritan threw my bag on the overhead rack.

When I sank into the aisle seat, the only empty one in sight, my seatmate's head rolled over to rest on my shoulder. Hands from above and behind grabbed the bristly blond head and yanked the inert body over to the window side.

"Don't mind George," a smiling youth said. "He's a sleeper."

I felt sure the young sleeper wouldn't respond to an om shanti but I took his name to be an omen, a good omen, that the right George would be waiting for me in New York.

Just arriving at the station was a treat. Tramps, carts, straggling families, kids with bulging knapsacks, and crisp CEOs running for trains to Greenwich or Syosset—those sights and the excitement the announcers offered. The Montrealer, now boarding; the Broadway Limited bound for the west on track nine. The only other people I heard speaking English were the beggars.

The current influx of cab drivers in the city have a maddening way of not acknowledging one's directions. My turbanned driver was no exception, and drove me at breakneck speed to stop three long blocks away from Kay's building. It was no pleasure tipping the man—a reminder that the wonderful Big Apple is no piece of pie.

Kay's apartment on Bleecker Street was every kid's dream of the perfect pad for that first step toward the stage, the podium, the publisher's office, or an art gallery. It was no fun walking up the stairs to get there. The fun was opening the door and walking across the room to the windows that overlooked Ashcan School backyards to the top of the Empire State Building glimmering in the city's awesome dusk.

Kay had a substantial year-round house in the Hamptons. This one-room flat was her urban roost. Opposite the windows, a dinky bathroom hid behind one door. A louvered door revealed the kitchen, which featured a stove, a tiny refrigerator, and a sink the size of a top hat.

India prints hung from a shower rod in a corner of the room. Not only did they conceal some clothing, they formed a linen closet and storage space and also held a jackknifed mattress that both Sophie and Hilary had used often when visiting. There was a convertible couch, a squishy chair, and Kay's drafting table. The walls were covered with fashion pinups and whole pages of magazines with hieroglyphic-type memos attached.

I put a vendor's hot dog in the toaster oven to warm up and assembled a Scotch and soda. Kay's desk chair hit my back in just the right spot as I sat at her dropleaf table to pore over the Yellow Pages. There were more than twenty places listed under Yoga. Six were in the Village or in SoHo. Two were familiar. One was my favorite, an immaculate, well-run establishment that I went to anytime I had a few spare hours in the city. I decided that my serious investigation should begin in the morning, though I toyed with the idea of checking on the nearest yoga address. Maybe a walk around the block would be good for my knee. I tried to remember the oft-repeated advice from my medical expert, Jane Brody, in *The New York Times*. RICE was the acronym for the proper treatment for battered joints. R stood for rest. I'd done that last night. I for ice. I'd done that too; and what the hell did C stand for? I tried out a dozen words beginning with C that didn't work. E, I knew, meant exercise. But since I hadn't done whatever C was, I figured I'd sit tight.

Hilary called before I turned in, and we chattered for half an hour. He said that Gray had called on him and told him about Butler's questioning Sophie about her tennis match the day her house was blown up and what, he wanted to know, was that all about?

Being a bit of a Pollyanna, I'm inclined to let dark thoughts drift out of my mind. I realized that because it was inconceivable to think of Sophie as devious or a liar, I had never talked to her about her actions that day.

"Why don't you ask her yourself, Hil? Then tell me. You know Sophie. When she's engaged with a hot new beau, as she was with Sid, at least half of her brain cells close down."

When I put down the phone I had to ask myself why in the world Gray would have told Hilary anything that cast doubt on Sophie.

I had no answers. My own brain cells were crying for sleep.

After a wrestling match with Kay's yank-out bed, its premasticated sheets and gnawed blanket looked like heaven.

When I woke up the next day I thought about long-gone blues singer Moms Mabley, who said of old age: "You wakes up one morning and you knows you got it."

I had it, all right. When I made it to the bathroom, the mirror on the back of the door told me that not only did I have it, but it showed. Half of my rear end looked like a tropical storm about to happen. The rest of my backside displayed other assorted black-and-blue spots. Fortunately I couldn't examine my front because it was impossible to turn around without falling over the toilet.

The first yoga establishment I visited that morning was on West Tenth Street. It occupied the first two floors of a shabby brownstone. I was charmed by the ferret that was curled up in a basket on the harvest table in the front hall. After taking me in with one quick glance, the ferret proceeded with his nap.

I examined all the pamphlets and brochures on the table until a young woman in white sweats appeared.

"Cute." I pointed to the ferret. "Is it friendly?"

"Schwarzenegger? Oh, yeah. She likes to sleep after breakfast."

"George," I said, exuding confidence. "I'd like to speak to George, please."

"George? He got a last name?"

"I hate to admit I've forgotten it. Is there anyone named George here? A student? Teacher?"

"Don't know. A lot of people take new names. Sanskrit names."

"Hey." Another young woman, as blond as her friend was dark, looked around the corner. "Heard you. How about George Rouse. You know."

"Oh, yeah, that's right. He's got flu or something. He's not here."

She gave me George's address, let me pat Schwarzenegger, who winked at me, and we said goodbye.

An infusion of hope made me straighten up. Swinging my stick, I marched along humming the Marseillaise.

When I was buzzed in to another unloved brownstone, I considered that I may have uncovered the meaning of the letter C. It must be for climb. When I knocked on George's door I felt sure it would reveal an apartment the size of Kay's.

When the door opened, I could hardly distinguish the rumpled bum who was standing there from the murky mess behind him.

"Don't come in. It's too awful in here." The hall light revealed a young, unshaven, tousle-haired fellow with an engaging smile. "If you're from the Board of Health, lady, I give up. I'll go quietly."

"Before I intrude on your"—I almost said squalor—"privacy, please answer one question for me. Have you ever been to India?"

He croaked. Maybe it was a laugh. "Yes, ma'am. Have you ever been to Pago Pago?"

"Yes, I have." My spirits soared. George had been to India. George needed me; I needed him. "In, in." I pushed him back inside. I strode over to the window and pulled it open. I picked up a ghastly mess of bedclothes and threw them over the windowsill to air.

George Rouse looked dazed and watched me with a rather sweet silly smile. Maybe he was in a drug-induced state. At least he hadn't dashed over to throw me out the window or dial 911.

"I'll bet you are from the Board of Health." He stood wiggling his bare toes and scratching his head.

"May I?" I didn't wait for a reply. I opened the refrigerator door. Inside was a bunch of limp carrots, a carton of whipping cream, a jar of capers, strawberry jam, and mustard.

"Hey, I'm embarrassed." He hugged himself. "It's not always this bad. I've been sick."

"Been sick. Now it's time to shape up." I have no idea what someone from the Board of Health does, but George seemed sweet and docile and I felt like the lady on the Dutch Cleanser can. Besides, I was curious to see what George really looked like.

"First, please shave and take a shower. I am going to get some food and you are going to re-enter the world of the living."

George yelled at me as I went downstairs. "What's your name?"

"Just call me Saint Letitia. Hurry. I'll be back soon."

When I returned I was accompanied by a strong young Pakistani, son of the owner of the convenience store where I had stopped for George. He groaned under the load.

In my zeal I managed to spend more than fifty dollars, but George's appreciative response made it worth the money.

"Now," I said, as we were putting marmalade on huge bran muffins, "tell me about India."

"Okay. Let's see." George's face scraped clean was pale, his eyes very blue, his hair wet and shiny black, his bones well arranged, and his expression cheerful. "Let's see. My father was with the State Department beginning in, let's see, I think I was seven, but I don't remember."

My head fell forward. I held it with my hands. I should have known better than to let my hopes rise. You old fool.

I must have said it out loud. I looked into his wide-open eyes. "You don't know Sid Colt?"

"Sorry, never heard of him. You know, there are some good books about India." He looked puzzled, with reason. I felt that I owed him at least a simple explanation of my behavior and of my quest.

George laughed. "You're not from the Board of Health. If I'd told you I'd never been to India I'd be in the same awful mess. I sure thank you."

George insisted I give him my address and said that someday he wanted to come put something wonderful in my refrigerator. A little later, we parted like old friends.

Back at Kay's, I brewed tea and made myself call the other numbers listed under Yoga. One number had been disconnected and none of the other places knew anyone called George.

My era was full of forthright square names. I grew up with lots of Georges and Johns and Henrys—names that had been overcome by made-up names like Rock, Lee, and Hunt.

Hilary was right. Mine was a futile search. I poked around behind Kay's Indian print curtain and took a pair of black sweatpants off a hook. A restorative class at my favorite place seemed to be in order.

Once there, of course, I made inquiries about George—any George—but I displayed less confidence and little enthusiasm.

There wasn't a George on the staff, nor among the volunteer teachers. Most pupils, I was told, used initials or nothing.

Lying on the pale gray carpet before the class began, I thought of Moms Mabley again. After you've got it, she forgot to say, you lose something. In my case, energy. I was just plain tired. Ah well, I counted my blessings Pollyanna-style. I was here, isolated from the real world, safe and silent. I told myself to take a deep breath, two, three, exhale slowly, concentrate on the spot between my eyebrows. Melt into the floor. Let go. Without my glasses, I couldn't see the instructor except to realize that she was young and had long blond hair. Her mellifluous voice guided us through an hour of poses and stretches.

Yoga means a union of body and mind. The trick is not to think, and it's harder than you can imagine. That's why yoga classes are so popular. You're not home lying on your own rug looking at the dust under the couch or that damn crack in the

159

ceiling. At class you can concentrate on not thinking of anything and on doing only what the 'eader says. "Lace your fingers over your head. Point your toes to the opposite wall. Stretch.
Breathe. Press the small of your back on the floor and rise to a
seated position. Inhale, then exhale, bend over your knees. Relax your elbows; relax your head; breathe."

When our instructor intoned her last om shanti and the
class eased out of its trance, she announced that she would be
in the hall available for any questions. "My name," she said, "is
Georgia."

It's a good thing my endorphins had given me a sense of
serenity, or I would have screamed while waiting for three different students who lined up wanting to speak to her. The last
one, a furry little man, seemed to be asking her for a date. She
didn't act pleased, so I nudged him out of the way and introduced myself.

"I know we've met, Georgia. I'm trying to think where it
could have been or with whom."

On close examination Georgia looked rather coarse. Perhaps
it was the drift of fine blond hair that made her features suffer in
contrast. Her eye sockets were shallow and her nose was flat
and broad. She managed a minor smile, and what could she say
to my silly question?

"I know," I gushed. "I think I must have met you with Sid
Colt."

Her expression changed. She hadn't moved a muscle but her
eyes were alert and attentive.

"Sid who?"

"Colt. Sid Colt."

Georgia shook her head and looked down at her hands.
"Nope, sorry."

She started to move away when I said, "We're all sorry about what happened."

"What happened? Who? What do you mean?"

"Sid's dead. He was murdered last week in Vermont."

When she raised her head, what I saw in her eyes was panic, or maybe it was fear, but she said nothing.

If I had X-ray eyes I'm sure I could have seen her heart pounding.

She turned and walked quickly toward the stairs. I managed to grab her loose shirt.

"Please, take this." I had come down supplied with some old calling cards with my address and phone number. "Call me, please, if you think of anything—anything at all about Sid." She started up a stair and I grabbed again. "Do you know Graham Gray?" She shook her head, pulled away, and ran up the stairs.

I rushed down to the entry desk only to wait in line while a dozen people signed in for the next class.

Finally, face to face with the person in charge, a long-haired bespectacled guru in orange garments, I asked if he could tell me Georgia's address.

"Georgia, our Georgia who took the two-thirty class?" I nodded. "She lives right here in the building."

"Oh, that's right. It's silly of me but I've forgotten her last name."

"We don't use last names." The guru's attention was taken by the person behind me.

"So near and yet so far," I thought. Out loud, I guess, as the woman standing beside me gave me a there-but-for-the-grace-of-God-go-I look.

I remembered that residents of the yogic persuasion boarded

in dormitories on the top two floors, an area out of bounds for others. I knew it was hopeless to wait for Georgia Whatshername. Thanks to other exits she could avoid me with ease.

Using my sketch pad, I wrote a note which I gave to the guru to give to Georgia. A note imploring her to get in touch with me in Vermont or, failing that, to telephone Detective Butler.

EIGHTEEN

To make myself an honest woman in Butler's eyes, I had my hair cut in midtown, caught the 5:10 for Albany, and found my car undisturbed at the parking lot.

Driving more than an hour on a moonless Vermont night is not my cup of tea, so I checked into the first nice-looking motel I saw and called home. No answer. I called Hilary and got his machine, and told the damn thing to expect me for breakfast in the morning.

I got to Lofton before eight, and yelled hello into an empty house. A note on the newel post told me that Sophie and Lulu were at Hilary's.

Kicking off my boots and rumpled clothes, I eased into jeans and a flannel shirt, downed a handful of vitamins, and proceeded to Hilary's house, testing my knee with a very slow jog.

Lulu was ecstatic to see me, and Hilary beamed at my gift of boccacino, heavenly ovals of marinated mozzarella from Joe's on Sullivan Street.

Sophie made a charade of looking around. She even opened

the front door, peering outside. "Well, where's George?"

I ignored her and stood behind the chair to give Hil's shoulders a massage. "How are you, Hil?"

"Just great."

"Really? Great?"

"That's what Ruth says. That's what she told me this morning when she left. Said lots of people needed her more than I did. But look what I've got instead. Sophie, my short-order cook."

"Will you take what you get for breakfast, Tish?" Sophie asked.

"Yes, ma'am. I'm starving."

"Okay, but not one single word about the New York toot till I get back."

Hil swooned under my strong hands. You can't stretch as many canvases as I have without getting powerful thumbs. I smiled over at our peaceable kingdom curled up on the couch.

"Hey," Hilary said, "what's the matter?"

"Did I shudder? I was thinking about the rattlesnake. I don't think I can ever sit on that couch again."

"You don't have to, Letitia. I'll get a new one."

There's a lot to be said for a man who knows when to take you seriously.

Sophie came back with a well-appointed tray featuring a poached egg on toast that was barely visible under a pile of crisp bacon, a pretty bowl of melon balls, and a fat Quimper coffeepot filled to the brim.

She then arranged herself on the couch with the animals. "We'll wait," she said. "Ugh. Hil, may I have your permission to vacuum Vanessa? These hairs get to me."

I didn't hear Hilary's reply. I was transported to the scene a few days ago when I removed hairs from Gray's shoulders—not Lulu hairs, my assumption at the time, but Vanessa hairs. I'd think about it later.

With many interruptions, I told them about my trip in chronological order.

Where, Sophie wanted to know, did one get a ferret?

Hilary said he didn't approve of wildlife as pets, and they took off into a long argument. They both got a laugh out of my Board of Health Lady Bountiful act with tousled George Rouse. Sophie demanded a precise description of his looks, and decided he sounded cute.

The drama I tried to add to my discovery of Georgia didn't impress my listeners.

"Georgia, not George." Hil shook his head. "That's really reaching, Tish."

They both threw cold water on my opinion that Georgia knew Sid.

"She denied knowing him," Hilary said. "Only the expression in her eyes made you think otherwise?"

"Yes. And after her surprise, she tried to get away. I had to actually grab her."

"She may have taken you for someone else," Sophie said. "Like maybe her new boyfriend's batty grandma."

"Gee, thanks, dear. But I just don't think your heart-warming assessment is correct. I'm going to call Butler."

I left them nattering once again about ferrets and desacked skunks and pet boa constrictors.

Sitting on the edge of Hilary's bed to telephone made me uneasy. I could see Sid curled over on his own blanket of blood.

Detective Butler wasn't in. I left word for him to call me at home.

Walking around the bedroom, I touched familiar objects. What had the killer done after he murdered Sid? Dashed out? Or maybe cautiously looked out the windows? We'd been told there were no prints on Hil's poker, and it was hard to imagine that the murderer, in his anger or haste to kill with the closest weapon, would be wearing gloves. He must have wiped away his prints.

Something bothered me about the room. Some subtle change. Possibly Ruth had moved something, but no change was apparent to me.

"I'm going home, Tish." Sophie leaned around the open door. "Coming?"

Still frowning, I asked Hil to come in and look. Did he see anything different in the room?

"Nope." The room looked smaller as he stood, arms akimbo, frowning at the walls. "Ruth really had at it. Looks fine to me. Why?"

Shaking my head was enough of an answer. I was suddenly overcome with weariness, and had an overwhelming urge to go home and curl up with Lulu on the library couch, cover us both with Grandma Bray's afghan, and, with luck, pass out.

The move into my cocoon, however, was postponed by an unfortunate exchange with Sophie. Back at home I told Sophie I was thinking about Gray.

"What about him?"

"I must ask Butler if he has explored Gray's background. At the time Sid was killed, I remember plucking hairs off Gray's jacket and apologizing for Lulu's shedding, but today I realize the hairs were long—not Lulu's but Vanessa's. I mean, what do we know about the man?"

"Oh come on, Tish. Gray didn't even know Sid till a while

ago. Why would he kill him? That's a crazy thought."

I suggested she might be a little blinded by her fondness for him. "You two are getting pretty cozy, aren't you?"

"Cozy, whatever that means. Damn it, Tish, can't you stop being a snoop for ten whole seconds? I've heard you say that it's naive to judge others by yourself. But that's exactly what you're doing to me. You think I leap into the sack with every half-assed joker who rides into town. Well, for your information, Graham Gray is quite safe. He doesn't appeal to my lustful tastes. I'm going down to breathe some fresh air at the barn." The screen door sounded like a pistol shot at her exit.

I felt as though I'd been kicked in the belly. Was that what Sophie thought of me? I didn't know whether to laugh or cry. I resisted a temptation to call Hil and whine, to get a little sympathy about Sophie's sharp tongue. Didn't she know I was trying to help? She and Elvira Wyman should get together.

Before I could work up a real case about ungrateful youth and poor old Aunt Tish, Detective Butler, who had adopted my friends' yoo-hoo greeting, came barging through the door.

"Sorry, really sorry, but I have a favor to ask. The Millers are back."

"The Millers? How come?"

"The cops tagged them. They had a fender-bender in Wilkes-Barre, so we were notified. I talked to them. They said they'd come back on their own. Said they had been planning to anyhow. They've arrived, but the favor: Can I talk to them in here?"

"You certainly can—with me present." Butler left to get the Millers while I made coffee and put a package of small doughnuts on the table. I could feel a tingle of excitement. The Millers must know more than they had told anyone about Sid.

Bringing Wanda and Jake into focus as I scuttled around the

167

kitchen, I realized how little I knew about them. It was easy to become so wrapped up in one's own life that two human beings living three hundred yards away were strangers. None of us who was responsible for the store found the Millers prepossessing. We were just grateful they were innocuous and competent.

We greeted each other with handshakes. Jake, with his head lowered, mumbled apologies. Wanda, impassive, carried a chic Nantucket basket over one arm. My eyes made a frantic search of her person for any evidence of a protruding flute. I had a ghastly vision of her piping a cobra out of its lair.

They all accepted coffee, and Lulu dashed around trying to make everyone feel at home.

Jake cleared his throat. "We were waiting, Mrs. McWhinny—waiting until the police found out who killed Sid Colt. We were afraid."

"Cowards," Wanda said. "What we were is cowards."

Butler waved his notebook and advised the Millers to go back and start at the beginning. "Did you come to Lofton in the first place because of Sid Colt?"

"No," Wanda said most emphatically. "No. We had no idea he was anywhere near here. We hadn't even seen him in maybe four years. We answered the ad for country store managers."

"When you saw him four years ago, was your relationship cordial?" I asked.

Butler didn't look too pleased at my intercession, but said nothing.

"Cordial?" Jake seemed to come alive. "Our relationship has never been what you'd call cordial. Take a mean bully, who's cordial?"

Butler wanted to know about their feelings about Sid when they met in Lofton.

"We'd been happy working here for almost a month when Colt walked in. I didn't kill him—you've got to believe that—or we wouldn't have come back."

Butler looked skeptical. "But you wanted to kill him. Why? Just 'cause he was a bully?"

Wanda got up. "Can I use your, your facilities?"

I pointed to the library bathroom.

"You see," Jake spoke quickly, "years ago Sid Colt got Wanda pregnant. She had a botched abortion. We weren't married yet, but I wanted to kill him then, all right. I'm glad someone else did. Wait a minute, I'm not through yet. It's what I did do, and why we came back." He looked at Butler. "We really were going to come back. What I did do, I did dynamite Sophie's house."

Butler and I both reacted, but I don't know what we said. Wanda came back in at the same time, sat down calmly, and said, "I hate to hear Jake even tell about it."

"Slowly now, Miller," Butler said. "Tell me all—and I mean all—about it."

"In the store one day I was on my knees behind the cold counter taping some loose wires when I heard Sid say to someone in a low voice, 'I put it in his garage.' Then he laughed. I got up and whoever he was talking to was gone. I think it was that Mr. Gray. But later when I was still thinking about what he said, I went out and poked around in the garage. You know we kept the car outside. We used the garage—a good dry building—for storage, and that's where I found the case of dynamite. I wouldn't have believed it, except that Colt was so rotten mean he'd do anything. It was well hidden. I didn't tell Wanda."

No one said a word.

"The very next day I came into the front of the store and

there's Colt; he's got Wanda pushed against the wall."

"The slob was all over me like a giant jellyfish," Wanda said. "I bit his tongue and he hit me. When he left I had to hold onto Jake. Thank God he didn't have the butcher knife in his hand."

Jake sighed and resumed the narration. "For three years I worked in an excavating company. You know—foundations, basements. We used dynamite all the time. I know the stuff. One day your niece was talking to Wanda. She says, 'For two cents I'd blow up my house. I'd like to build on the other side of the road.'

"That gave me the idea. Frame Colt. I knew because of the tagnets they'd trace the dynamite to the quarry. I mean, the Feds are really careful of that stuff. Most people knew—I don't know if you did, Mrs. McWhinny—that Colt had sort of moved in on Sophie. I figured he'd be blamed."

I was stunned. That such a tepid person could do something so violent seemed impossible. If there was ever anyone who was called and couldn't come it was Jake Miller.

"You can be sure he didn't tell me. Crazy thing to do." Wanda glared at Jake.

"Go on, Mr. Miller," Butler said.

"So I took half a dozen sticks from the case, taped them up, and stuck in the detonator. Fixed the det wire and put the stuff and a plunger in my tool bag, and put it in the trunk of the car. Next day I heard Sophie say she's going to Dorset. Wanda's going to have her hair cut, driving in with Millie. So I call the quarry. Sid's not there. Might be in a couple of hours. Perfect. So I drive down and set the sticks under the gas tank. Run out with the wire and just as I jump in the car, set the stuff off. I'm back outside the store in less than three minutes. Marion, who was helping out, never even knew I left. And that, so help me, officer, is the God's truth. I'd never touched the hair of Sid Colt's head."

Wanda said, "Amen. He doesn't have to tell you why we ran out. When Mrs. McWhinny told me Sid was dead I knew we were in deep trouble, and we both thought it would be better to hide until you found the murderer. And, mind you, I didn't even know then that Jake had blown up Sophie's house. I just knew where Sid was there would be trouble, and you all knew we all came from Scranton. We stayed in my aunt's cabin in the mountains, and we'd about decided to come back to Lofton when we had the accident."

"Did you know Graham Gray before you came here?" I asked.

"Nope."

Butler asked Jake about the dynamite strung up to Hilary's house.

"We all watched the demolition truck, but nobody really knew what it was all about. Listen, I like Mr. Oats. I wouldn't do such a thing. When the truck left, Sophie called Wanda about the rattler, and I never did have time to check on the rest of the box of dynamite. We took off. Now I wish we hadn't. When they traced the stuff I was hoping it would get Sid in trouble. But"—he raised his palms—"don't think I killed him."

"If Jake killed him I'd know," Wanda said. "And I know he didn't." She made the pronouncement as though she had the last word on the matter and the case was closed.

The detective said he wanted Jake to go along with him to Rutland. Jake agreed. "Anything you want, officer."

"Can Mrs. Miller stay here with you, Mrs. McWhinny?"

I wanted to scream. "Not possible. Sorry, my niece is staying here and my sister and her husband are arriving soon." I don't even have a sister, but the idea of padding around the house with dour Wanda made me sick.

"Hey, no problem," Wanda said. "They said no one was in our old apartment. We left behind plenty of stuff. I'll stay there." I didn't say "thank goodness," but it must have been written on my face.

Nineteen

After the explosion Sophie had had a telephone installed in the barn, so I knew I could reach her there. But first I needed ten minutes to compose myself. I stretched out in a patch of sunshine on the carpet and did some deep slow breathing. I may even have gone to sleep. In any event, I rose refreshed.

Sophie registered amazement rather than anger when I told her about Jake.

"I'm glad he blew it up. The insurance company may not feel the same way. They were going to give me twelve thousand dollars more than it was worth. But that will be his business now."

She was relieved, too, that she was off the hook. "I want to see that one-cell cop on his knees. Tell him I'll be waiting, the bastard." She hung up.

Hilary had almost the same reaction, but wanted to know if I thought Jake had set the dynamite at his house or murdered Sid.

"I believe him, Hil. In fact I've put him out of my mind. We've got to find out about Gray." I told him about the Vanessa

173

hairs on Gray's sweater. He wasn't very impressed.

"I just came upon my old blow torch," he said. "So I think I'll make a baked Alaska tonight."

"Good God, Hil, you'd think someone got murdered in your bedroom every day. Nothing more on your mind than a baked Alaska."

"Can't think of anything I'd rather have on my mind. And how about some deep-fried eggplant fingers, crisp outside and soft and delicious inside? Why don't you ask Sophie?"

"She may be mad at me." I told him what she'd said.

"She thinks you're a bed-hopper. I want to hear more about that. Why not ask Gray, too. It'll give you a chance to detect him, while he's wallowing in meringue."

We all wallowed in Hil's gauzy concoction a lot earlier than I liked to have dinner. Sophie and Gray wanted to go to the movies, and good-natured Hil cooperated.

Gray was his agreeable self. He said Sophie had told him that my trip to New York was in vain, as I met a Georgia instead of a George.

Short of asking Gray a direct question—like, "Did you kill Sid?"—I couldn't think of anything I could ask that would be illuminating.

Sophie was pensive, and it was a relief when they left.

Hil talked me into an anisette with my espresso. Sitting there while Hilary gave me a blow-by-blow description of the afternoon he had spent with our private plumber, I had a flash of déjà vu—much the same sensation I had had in Hilary's bedroom after breakfast that morning.

Hil stood with his back to the fireplace. He looked like an ad for a lowland single-malt Scotch.

"I know what's wrong." I laughed.

"Wrong? With me?"

"Not you, dear heart. Behind you. I've never seen your barkentine look so serene."

"Oh, that." He turned around and poked one end of the painting. "I saw Gray straightening it when I was in the kitchen." The ship once again challenged the waves.

"That's it!" I jumped up and dashed into the bedroom. I yelled at Hilary, "What's Ruth's number?"

She was home. "Ruth, I'm at Hilary's. Tish. When you were here, of course you cleaned the bedroom. But think. Did you straighten those two pictures—the landscape over the mantel or that big dark one between the windows?"

"Naw. Why bother? They're always on the fritz, like that sailboat of his. He likes it that way."

"That's it, Hil. Oh, wow, that's it!"

"You're dithering. *What's* it?"

"Gray is the murderer. He couldn't help it. He straightened your paintings. He's a compulsive straightener-upper. It's irresistible. He has to line things up."

Before Hilary could tell me I was crazy or applaud my perspicacity I was dialing Butler. I knew his home number.

After I told him my theory, he asked some questions.

Did I know if Gray had ever been in the bedroom?

"Hilary," I called, "has Gray ever been in here, except the dinner when he first came, and last night?"

"Don't think so, but you said he was here right after the murder. I didn't see him go into the bedroom tonight, but I suppose he could have."

Butler asked me to call him after I talked to Sophie.

"Hey, don't hang up yet. If Sophie says Gray did not go into the bedroom, will you send someone down to take fingerprints

175

from the paintings? I know prints will show on those smooth frames."

Butler made it clear that my news could wait, and suggested we discuss the matter the next morning. "Don't call me. I won't be in the office."

It was only a little after eight when I got home, so I decided to call Elvira and tell her about Jake. I didn't think Butler spent much time relieving anyone's anxieties.

Edgar Wyman answered the phone. I lied and told him I realized he had never been a serious suspect, but knew he'd be glad to hear that Jake Miller had confessed to blowing up Sophie's house using the quarry's dynamite that Sid had placed in the store's garage.

Wyman didn't say anything, so I plowed on. "Please tell Elvira that when all this is behind us, I look forward to sketching with her again."

It wasn't difficult to imagine the four-letter words she might choose from to greet my message.

I didn't hear Sophie come in, and we didn't meet until breakfast. She was taking her last gulp of coffee as I poured my first cup.

I expected her to bristle at my question.

"Did Gray go into Hil's room?" she echoed my words. "No. Why would he do that?"

"You're sure?"

"Of course I'm sure. Honestly, Tish, you're going around the bend."

With that she rinsed out her cup and, before leaving, said, "By the way, Gray and I are going to Woodstock for lunch, and I'm expecting a call from the county inspector. Will you please tell him I'll be at the barn all day tomorrow?"

When Butler called, I was both excited and frightened. Sophie was having lunch with a murderer, I told him, and it was urgent that we identify his prints.

Butler didn't think he could send anyone down to Lofton to take prints today, but said he'd see that the paintings got to the lab if I could deliver them in Rutland. I must say, to his credit, that he expressed interest when I told him about the Vanessa hairs and where I found them.

As soon as I was dressed, I raced up to Hilary's with green lawn bags and a roll of tape. With his bum arm he couldn't help me, so he watched as I teetered on a stepladder, removing the pictures by handling only the top of the frames. I taped the bags and put them in the Trooper.

"Why don't I come with you, Tish?"

"I'd love it, but you wouldn't approve of what I'm going to do on the way back."

"Like?"

"Like poking around Gray's place."

"Around? You mean inside the man's house, right?"

I nodded. "The prints I expect to find on the frames may not be enough to suit Butler. I'd like some solid proof. God knows what. There must be something. Remember the night Sid showed us slides of India? Gray said he had some, and I got to wondering if they might tell us something."

"Sophie's no longer suspected of blowing up her own house, so why not leave it to Butler? Back off."

"It may surprise you to learn that I'm not keen about losing you. Whoever bumped you into the pit, he was right behind you and doesn't know you didn't see him."

"Why would I keep it a secret if I knew who it was?"

"My guess is that he might think it will come to you. That

you'll recall something that will trigger your memory and you'll be able to identify him, her, or it."

Hilary paced around the driveway, pulling on his left earlobe, which usually indicated deep thought.

"All right, I'll go. Somebody's got to look after you. We'll take my car. It's been fixed. Yours stands out like a sore thumb. I'll park outside his house and deflect any questions from whomever might stop. Say that my car's busted or something. Give you time to sneak away. Oh God, what am I saying? This is illegal trespass. I'm insane. We can't do this, Tish."

"I can, Hil. You don't have to come."

"What'll you do, break in?"

"You know I have everybody's key in Lofton. I've shown the house a couple of times for Fay's prospective tenants. Fingerprints!" I exclaimed. "Butler will have to have Gray's fingerprints for comparison. I'll snitch something from his house— or how about his wine glass from last night?"

"Ruth's coming this morning, so I didn't wash the dishes."

We both trotted over to the kitchen and stood looking at the array of glasses. If last night had been a standard Oats dinner party, there would be dozens of glasses of every shape and size.

Hilary picked up a wine glass. "Here's Gray's glass. Gray had the chardonnay, we had red, and Sophie was drinking beer."

Unrolling a yard of paper towel, I wrapped the glass and tucked it into a small shopping bag.

"Keep your fingers crossed," I said.

"You want Gray to be guilty. I thought you liked him. I think you're sort of ghoulish, Tish."

"I'll tell you one more time, Hil." I was getting tired of being the big bad wolf. "Someone wants you dead, and that someone thinks you may realize who it is."

In tight-lipped silence, I took the paintings out of my car and stood them upright against Hilary's back seat. "Shall I drive?" All cars seemed like racy sports cars after driving the Trooper. Even Hilary's old sedan. I rather enjoyed the trip to Rutland, and we managed to deliver the paintings to Butler.

On the way back, Hilary said he refused to dwell on my imminent unlawful project. Instead, he suggested that we discuss where we'd go when we could say goodbye to the present horridness.

Greece or Turkey appealed to me. A slow boat along the coast or a car driven by someone else. But the truth of the matter is, nice as it was to travel with Hilary, I really didn't want to go anyplace. How could anyone look at our gorgeous Vermont fall and think of going anywhere else? (Except, of course, during Vermont's two bad seasons, hunting and mud.) My work had suffered, too, and I was eager to close the door of my studio and just be there. Serving as an outpost for the police department, short-order cook, and coffee shop attendant was getting to be a pain in the neck.

"Back to the subject, Tish, I've got to tell you that there's no reason for suspecting Gray. It's all in your head."

"Not so. I think the fingerprints will prove he was in the room at the time Sid must have been murdered."

Hilary sniffed. "If and maybe."

"Why do you think Sid was murdered right after he sold the quarry? I know, because somehow Gray made a deal with Sid. I just know in my bones they're connected. And besides, who else could it have been? Don't say Jake; I don't believe it."

Hilary shrugged and shook his head and said nothing.

When we got to Gray's place Hilary put on a deep frown, and I exhaled a tremendous sigh.

For the fifth time, Hilary issued instructions. "If anyone stops, friend or foe, I'll honk once and you go out the back door and hide behind the garage. I'll wait . . ."

"Okay. I know, I know."

Hilary wished me luck and gave me a thumbs-up. I told him to be patient. When I gave him the finger, he quit scowling long enough to laugh.

The front door opened directly into the sunny living room, which made my devious ways seem doubly sleazy.

A pine harvest table with a couple of in-out boxes and a letter rack served as a desk for Fay's tenants. It had been organized by the same hand that lined up my silver. Everything was orderly, and in minutes I flipped through all the things that were none of my business.

There was a local checking account with a healthy balance. A quick look at his checkbook showed it had no unusual entries or withdrawals. What I really wanted to find were his slides, and they weren't on the desk.

I poked around behind his stereo equipment and felt behind Fay's tidy array of books. In the kitchen I yanked out drawers that were filled with the obvious, and I bent over to look in and under cabinets. Nothing. I trotted upstairs and looked in drawers—all immaculate and arranged in such military exactitude that no more than a glance was needed. There was only one suitcase in Gray's closet, and it was empty. Then I saw a leather briefcase hanging on a hook. I turned it upside down and was rewarded by a box of slides.

The box held only four frames. I don't know what I expected to find. One by one I held them up to the window, but without some enlargement it was hopeless. All I could make out were robed figures against an exotic background.

A voice just inches behind me said hello. If the windows had been opened I might have fallen out! I was so frightened I slid to my knees, making excruciating contact with the hardwood floor. The pill was yet to be made that could have slowed my hammering heart.

Hands grasping both my arms helped me rise to another shock. Georgia—Greenwich Village Georgia—was peering into my eyes.

"Are you all right? I didn't mean to scare you. I didn't know what to do. Oh dear, I shouldn't have come so close."

I knew what it must feel like to be in a nursing home as she led me to a chair.

Leaning back, I brought Georgia into focus. "You *do* know Graham Gray. My Lord, you wasted no time getting here. How did you manage?" Then I said rather fiercely, "Speak to me."

"The bus, the bus. Then I look a taxi to the store opposite your house in Lofton and I asked them where Greg lived, and the driver left me here. Greg was leaving when I got here and he told me to wait, that he'd be back about three."

"Greg?" I asked.

"Gray. He likes Gray better, I forgot."

"So you do know him. And how about Sid Colt?"

"I'm sorry, I promised Greg, Gray. He said not to say anything to anyone at all. He told me to stay out of sight. I saw you coming upstairs. I hid, but I knew it wouldn't work."

"You'd better come home with me right now, Georgia."

"Thanks, but I wouldn't dare."

We looked at each other for a minute. Her face was pale. She looked tense and wary. It was impossible to recall her as the poised, serene leader of a yoga class.

"Did Gray, or Greg, kill Sid Colt?"

"He wouldn't kill anyone. I'm sure of it."

"But you all knew each other?"

"Yes—I mean, no. I knew Gray in India. And we didn't do anything wrong. I mean really wrong. Listen, I can't tell you any more. I'll be in serious trouble."

"How would Gray cause trouble? Did he threaten you?"

"Of course not. But he is serious, and I just won't say another word."

"I'll have to tell the police about you."

"I don't know why. I haven't done anything that would interest the police here."

Of course she was absolutely right, and Butler would ask the same question: Why?

"Maybe we should keep this meeting to ourselves," I suggested. "Don't tell Gray. I won't tell anyone. We haven't met, okay? I hope I'm doing the right thing. Good luck and be careful. Remember, somebody killed Sid."

Georgia couldn't have seen me pocket Gray's slides. I could hardly wait to get home to examine them. Going down the stairs, I felt a tingle of elation to know that Gray had been in India. Maybe it wasn't, as Hil had said, all in my head.

Hilary had the engine running when I got in the car.

"You're really limping. What did you do, fall downstairs? Looks like you saw a ghost."

Hilary's slightly jeering questions were his way of punishing me for my criminal foray.

"Sort of. Don't ask, Hil. Please, just hurry home."

His undistinguished little car ate up the two miles in as many minutes. Hilary was understandably perplexed and annoyed when I urged him to leave me and go on home. But I did promise to call him later.

TWENTY

Where was Butler when I needed him? It was Saturday and I supposed the man was entitled to some time off. I left word for him to call me.

There was a good chance I might go mad between now and three o'clock, when Gray was supposed to reappear. And Sophie—was she safe or had Gray stopped to show her Quechee Gorge?

I ransacked the library before I found my small slide enlarger. I pulled up a chair by the window.

I've never been to India, but it was clear that that is where the pictures had been taken. Of the four slides in the box, it was the last slide that made me feel sick to my stomach. The picture showed what seemed to be a very old man swathed in flowing garments lying on the ground. Kneeling on one knee behind him was Sid Colt with his hand on what might have been the handle of a knife protruding from the man's back. Was I imagining it or did Sid look like a hunter proud of his kill? Had Gray been blackmailing Sid?

I was sitting in a trance when Sophie blew in. "How do you like my new hat?" She twirled around, displaying a becoming lavender Irish tweed hat. "What's with you, Tish? You look sort of droopy."

"I'm not droopy. I'm terrified. Did you go by Gray's house?"

"Nope. Came in by way of Londonderry. He had to stop at the bank. Why?"

"Oh God. Did Gray say anything about someone being at his house?"

"Yes. But how did you know that? Said someone was there and he was going to show his friend around these parts."

"Where? Where around these parts?"

"Hey, cool it. He didn't say."

"Think. Think!" I guess I shook her.

She held the sides of her head. "He said he thought Route 4 from Rutland to Fair Haven was one of the great drives, and maybe—he did say something about the quarries? Like they were an unusual sight for tourists. Or maybe that was yesterday."

I ran to the phone and dialed Butler's home and talked to a young boy who said his dad would be home soon. I left a message.

Sophie watched me frantically paw through my phone book and dial a number. Thank God Elvira answered. "Elvira—this is so important, please, life and death. Are they working at the quarry today?"

She said thanks to some rainy days during the week, yes they were. But she said they'd be quitting soon.

"This sounds crazy, but they have to keep working. At least get Wyman to stay there—have some trucks moving around. I haven't time to explain."

I closed Lulu in the kitchen and yelled at Sophie. "Get my gun. Beside my bed." Sophie was a sharpshooter and responsible for keeping my small .22 target pistol in working order. She had caught the urgency and wasted no time asking questions.

"You coming with me?"

"You gotta be crazy, me let you go off alone with a gun?"

We ran outside. Sophie, without a by-your-leave, got in the driver's seat of the Isuzu and we nearly ran over sweet Charlie as we shot out of town.

"Where are we going?"

"First by Gray's." In less than three minutes we passed his house. "No sign of a car. On to the quarry."

During our hair-raising trip, I told Sophie everything that had transpired since last I'd seen her, and told her what I thought might happen.

"You see, Gray must have killed Sid to keep his share of the money."

"What money?"

"Gray was blackmailing Sid, don't you see? He took that picture of him kneeling beside the old man he killed. Maybe that's okay in some parts of the world, but not here, dear girl. Why, Gray could ruin his life, which Sid knew. So it seems obvious to me that Sid would have had to pay Gray a lot or part of the money he'd get for selling the quarry."

"Come on, Tish. You're telling me Gray would kill Sid for money?"

"Big money, the money Sid sent to Nassau."

"And this girl, Georgia, why harm her?"

"I don't know. Maybe she had some money coming to her. She looked pretty nervous."

"I don't believe it, any of it."

"So don't. If nothing's wrong at the quarry, well, no harm done. I mean, if we get there alive. I'll just look like a fool. So what's new?"

We drove the rest of the way, me wincing at every curve. Sophie had a firm grip on the wheel; her lower lip stuck out in a profile of obstinance.

We nearly ran over a woman carrying flowers away from the Saturday farmer's market in the Fair Haven town square. We left a stunned child holding his arm aloft. His balloon was stuck in our grill and bounced gaily on the hood.

It's difficult to make an invisible approach preceded by a red balloon. Sophie brought us to a skidding stop behind the first shed.

On foot, we wove around the sheds and ducked huge chunks of slate being moved by truck, and finally ran into Edgar Wyman.

"Hey, what's going on? I got this call from Elvira. She didn't know what you were talking about."

"Have you seen a man and a woman?"

"You mean Gray and a lady? Yeah, they're walking around the rim." He pointed toward the crater.

With a quick change of glasses, I could see the faraway figures.

"Tish thinks Gray's going to push his friend into the quarry," Sophie said derisively.

"With all of us watching? Really, Mrs. McWhinny." He shook his head.

"If I hadn't called Elvira, no one would be here, right? And it could have happened. Let's go out where they can see us and just wait for them."

"You still want the trucks to drive around?"

"Oh please, yes—at least till I can talk to them."

Wyman walked off to talk to a driver of one of the behemoths.

I locked my arm through Sophie's. "I know you think I'm nuts, but I beg you, please do as I say."

"Want me to shoot someone?" She looked mildly indulgent.

"Listen, when we meet up with them, Gray and Georgia, we'll just talk and talk until they act as though it's time to leave. Then is when I want you to say you have to go somewhere, too. You've got to go to see someone—a lawyer or a dentist in Granville. Take the Isuzu and leave quickly. I'll get them to drive me home. First phone you find, call Butler and tell him what happened and to come to Lofton. Dear God, I hope he's finished with those fingerprints."

"You want me to leave you with Gray when you've decided he's a murderer?"

"Don't ask. Please do as I say. Here they come."

In a long lifetime of greetings and partings, I've never felt as unwelcome as when I strode with outstretched hand toward Georgia and Gray. Sophie, with her buoyant good looks, must have been equally unaccustomed to such an expressionless reception.

Gray introduced Georgia. Georgia Krim, a friend from Florida. Georgia played it deadpan as I grasped her damp hand.

The depth of the quarry, its width, its history, the pay rate of the workers—there wasn't one bit of information I left undelivered in my endless stream of words. When I ran out of words, good loyal Sophie described the many uses of tile and even picked up shards from the ground for them to feel and examine.

Gray lacked his usual charm when he tried to smile, and

ended up with a grimace. They, he said, had to leave.

Sophie started for the car, calling out that she too had an urgent appointment.

"Hey!" Gray called after her. "Wait for your aunt."

Sophie waved as she started the car and noisily made her exit.

"Oh dear," I simpered. "I should have asked you first. I do hope you'll give me a lift back to Lofton."

There was much backing and filling and frowning, but Gray finally gave in. Wordlessly he opened the back door of the car, and I was barely inside when he slammed it shut.

Gray drove even faster than Sophie. I reviewed my life and decided it was greedy to want more time on this earth, and I tried desperately to think of other reasons to make sudden death more acceptable.

When I put a cold hand in my pocket, my fingers folded around the grip of my .22. I'd forgotten it was there, and I felt a surge of confidence. No one was going to learn anything by pussyfooting around. I squared my shoulders, took a deep breath, and asked Gray why he'd killed Sid.

We locked eyes in the rearview mirror. "You're crazy."

I'd been called crazy once too often lately. The word kindled my ire, firmed my resolve.

I repeated my question.

"This isn't like you, Tish."

"Oh yes, it's just like me." I hated his calling me Tish. I waved my .22 beside his head. "See? You're going to answer some questions. I'll use this if I must."

"You wouldn't dare."

"Assumptions are dangerous, Gray. And you"—I spoke to Georgia, who had been attending to our words like a tennis fan—"do you know if your friend here killed Sid?"

"Thank you," Gray said. "I can speak for myself. I didn't kill him, nor did I commit any other crime." He looked at Georgia and slowed down. "What did you tell her?"

"Nothing. I told you, we just said hello at your house. Nothing, honest."

"We discussed your time together in India," I said. "Didn't we, Georgia? So come on, Gray." I poked him with the gun. "Tell me about Sid." I never realized a tiny gun could give anyone such a feeling of power. "Let's hear it."

"Sid deserved what he got."

"Did Sid blow up Sophie's house?" I wanted to see if Gray would lie.

"No, he didn't."

"Did he loosen the lugs on Hilary's car?"

"Yes. And he brought the rattlesnake into the house. That would be just like him."

"Did he tell you why?"

"I knew why. He wanted Oats out of the way so Sophie could inherit the place right away."

"And the dynamite to Hilary's house, how about that?"

"I knew he was going to do that, but didn't realize he had, until Sophie discovered it."

"Why? Why?"

"Same reason he liked Lofton. He wanted to be king of the mountain, on the double."

"And you? Did you want to buy our general store to play king of the mountain, too?"

From the moment we got into the car, Gray's voice had lost its cozy, confidential tone. "I thought it would be fun to own the store while I was waiting . . ."

"For Sid to sell the quarry. Right?"

I hoped Gray could see my sneer in the rearview mirror. Did this traitor to the vanishing tribe of the mannerly think I'd believe anything he'd say now?

"Wrong," he said. "I was waiting for your niece to find out what kind of man Sid was."

It was a mistake, but I asked Gray why he hadn't said he knew Sid. "Or," I said, "shall I call you Greg?"

"None of your business." He turned to Georgia. "So you just said hello to Mrs. McWhinny?"

Then Gray slammed on the brakes. Georgia squealed as her head hit the dashboard, and I was catapulted forward with my shoulders wedged between the headrests. Gray grabbed a handful of my hair and shoved his other hand under me, nearly amputating my breast as he captured my gun.

He swung the car into a dirt road, stopped again, and, leaning across Georgia, opened the front door and gave her a brutal shove. I heard her gasp as she rolled out of sight.

Gray jumped out and opened my door and, with a grip on the lapel of my jacket, yanked me onto the road, pulled me around the back of the car, and pushed me into the ditch.

Poor Georgia. But thank God for her, she inadvertently broke my fall. On all fours, she must have been trying to get up when I tumbled on top of her.

Part of her long blond hair was a mass of burrs, and there was a long scratch across her cheek. She moaned and groaned, and I swore while we tried to untangle ourselves.

"Get up." Gray's hand grabbed my arm. "I've changed my mind. You're going to drive."

Anger overcame my fear; I was furious. "You rotten son of a bitch. To think I treated you like a friend." I tried to spit in his face with no success. I never could spit very well. Besides, he was busy pulling Georgia out of the ditch. He told her to get in front. She continued to moan while I kept on cursing the man. His image had undergone a radical change after shoving me ass-over-teakettle into the ditch. His whimsical eyebrows now assumed an evil arch. His once serene expression now appeared to be rigid and tense, and his quiet voice came across as controlled venom.

"I can't drive."

"Oh yes, you can." He tightened his grip on my arm. "Get in!"

"My glasses." I felt my head. "My glasses!"

I thought Gray might shoot me out of sheer impatience while I groped around in the briars and weeds trying to find them.

Georgia, who had come to my aid, found my specs intact and handed them to me with a trembling hand.

Silently we rearranged our positions, and after moving up the seat and examining the strange dashboard, I turned on the ignition and drove off once again on the macadam road.

Gray's face in the rearview mirror was drawn in thin horizontal lines. His eyes were slits, and his mouth without lips.

"I was right, wasn't I? I know what you were waiting for, Gray. When I saw your picture of Sid with the man he murdered in India, I knew then."

"Nobody murdered anybody. It was just a joke."

"Some joke. You were blackmailing Sid, and the day he sold the quarry and you knew the money had been sent to Nassau, you killed him."

The pressure I felt against my right shoulder was new to me, but I knew what it was. My system once again reversed itself and I was suddenly weak with fear. Even though I reasoned that

Gray wouldn't shoot, to have a gun—my gun—pressing into my flesh caused my foot to falter on the gas pedal. We might have gone off the road if Georgia hadn't grabbed the wheel.

With no religious intermediaries and not much faith in the practice, I prayed directly to Detective Butler. I hoped the frantic vibrations of my thoughts would lead him to us. You can drive for a month in Vermont without seeing a police car, so I guess I was asking too much.

I was still praying when we came to Gray's house, where he escorted us inside. "Straight ahead. Open that door, Georgia." She opened a door that led to the cellar. Gray held the back of my collar as he leaned over me to flick on the light. "Down."

TWENTY-ONE

I nearly fell as Gray pushed us both down the stairs. I caught one last look at him as he reached up and unscrewed the light bulb. The door shut and we heard what had to be a bolt sliding into its socket. The only light in the minuscule cellar came from a screened opening about the size of a carton of cigarettes. Outdoor furniture was stacked in half the space. The rest was occupied by the furnace and hot-water heater.

Grateful that the place was at least dry, I sank down on the stairs and bent over my miserable knee. Only concentrated deep breathing helped me unclench my jaws. I welcomed the momentary serenity of our cell.

Georgia's face was a mess. Her deep scratch had been bleeding, and there was blood all over her hands.

I folded the cotton scarf I'd worn into a rectangle and pressed it against her face. She seemed close to panic or shock, conditions I didn't feel capable of addressing, but I put my arm around her shoulders and cooed at her like someone soothing a baby. Gradually her shivering ceased.

I had to repress an urge to start battering down the door, but I thought Georgia had better collect herself first. We would need her youthful power. I didn't have what it takes to be a battering ram.

"He's going to kill us," she moaned.

"No, no, he's not. Calm down. You said he wasn't a killer. I mean, he may have murdered Sid, but there's no reason to do away with us. He's been running around upstairs. I've heard him—packing, I'll bet. There, listen, the car. He's leaving, the bastard. Come on now, tell me about him."

"You'll have to excuse me. I'm not usually such a crybaby. Greg said"—she mopped her face with the scarf—"Sid said, too, that there was nothing really wrong with what we did in Suriname. We just helped that guy Tilt with his rice sale. Greg figured out how to do it and made a deal that we'd be paid. They swore it wasn't against the law in the United States. Honest—or I wouldn't have done it."

Exasperated, I asked, "What actually did you do?"

The description Sid had given during his slide show of the activities in Suriname was slowly coming back to me.

"It was about a shipload of rice bought at below market price and sold to Holland for lots more, and this guy Tilt would make a huge profit, a few million. All he needed was the proper stamped sale document. Between the three of us we stole it. I actually picked it up off the desk—and we were to divide a hundred thousand dollars."

"We? You mean Sid, too?"

She nodded.

"Phew, good pay. Then what? Were you all in a deal to sell the quarry?"

"The quarry—no, it had nothing to do with the quarry. I

don't know anything about that except that we all went to Nassau to open a bank account for when Tilt paid off. Sid went by himself to see the agent about selling the quarry. Then he left for the States. I never saw him again; and Greg, Gray, and I flew home. We stopped in Atlanta where he wanted to arrange for an I.D. change."

"A what?"

"You know, change his name. Used to be Greg Gearon. It's like you go to a cemetery and find the grave of some little kid that died about twenty or thirty years ago. Then in New York Greg gets a drop address and, using the kid's name, sends for a copy of the birth certificate. And there you are."

"My Lord, then what do you do? How do you get a social security number and all that?"

"Let's see. He takes the certificate and the envelope it was mailed in to the bank and opens an account. Then he tells the Social Security people he's been living in England with his family and was a student and never had a job—or he said you could say you'd been nuts and in an institution—then you get a driver's license and a couple of credit cards and you're Graham Gray. It's called doing a Kilroy. The Feds do it all the time for scared witnesses."

"Why did he want to change his name?"

"He didn't actually tell me, but I gathered he was in India in the first place to escape from the huge alimony his wife had been awarded. And when we were in Miami, he said changing his name was so Greg Gearon could vanish, like die, just never come back from India. When we all used to talk about Sid's quarry a lot, Greg joked and called himself the elusive quarry."

"Did you see Sid kill the Indian man in the picture?"

"No, I don't know that they killed him. I had walked on

ahead. But I saw them pulling him into the bushes."

"Might Gray have killed him?"

"No. Sid could have. He was—what do you call them—
someone with no sense of right and wrong. And he could be
mean. Really mean. Do you think Gray would have killed me
at the quarry? Pushed me over the edge?"

I thought he might have. I shrugged. "I hope he's halfway to
Canada and I hope I never have to see him again in my life. I
trusted him. I feel like a stupid fool. But tell me, if you're afraid
of Gray, why did you come up here to Lofton?"

"The money. When you said Sid had been killed I was afraid
something might happen to my share of the money. The money
we were supposed to get from Tilt in Suriname."

"This Suriname business. I don't see what it's got to do with
anything."

"Like I told you, it doesn't, except for the money we get.
When we deposited it in Nassau we each kept fifteen thousand
and decided it would be fun to meet and divide the rest of it
two years from that day."

"How in the world did you get tied up with these guys in the
first place? Could you please start at the beginning?"

"Sid was my stepbrother."

"Your brother!" I suddenly saw myself as the straight man in
a grade B movie. I rubbed my eyes. "Now, in words of one
syllable, please, Georgia, fill me in. When and why did you and
Sid go to India together?"

"I had never ever laid eyes on Sid. Our mutual father died
when I was small and my mother remarried and we lived in
Bristol, Tennessee. Last spring I had a messy divorce and found
myself at loose ends and luckily was awarded a lump sum of
money. Then I got this urge to check out Sid. I can't remember

how, but I knew he still lived in Scranton and I found myself talking to his landlady. Seems he'd been in India maybe more than a year and she told me where she sent his mail—first two weeks in May in New Delhi and like that. I wanted to kick the traces and a little adventure appealed to me. So I camped out at the American Express in New Delhi and the second day he showed up."

"How did you know him?"

"Oh, I hung out by the counter and could hear people's names. Besides, he looked like the pictures of my father. It was easy, you know, joining up with other Americans, especially in India. I'd promised myself that no way was I going to tell him who I was till I was darn well ready."

"What was Sid like?"

"Charming, fun, and mean as a snake."

"And Gray, was he there then?"

"Oh, sure. They'd joined up a few months before. We got along fine. Took me a while to realize he was almost as mean as Sid but much smarter."

"If they were so mean why did you stay with them?"

"When I'd talk about leaving they'd urge me to stay, but actually I was sort of scared and had just about made up my mind to split when Sid got word about inheriting the quarry. You can bet that made me want to stick around and find out what might be in it for me."

"I wonder why Sid and Gray didn't say they knew each other here in Vermont," I asked Georgia.

"They didn't? Well, I guess it's because Sid liked center stage and Gray was trying to keep a low profile. I mean, he wouldn't want anyone saying, 'What were you doing in India?' Or, 'Don't I know you from someplace?'"

"What happened after Sid found out he owned a slate quarry?"

"Like I told you, we went to Suriname and then back in New York I got smashed one night and told Greg Sid and I had the same father. He didn't believe me and said I just wanted to get something out of the quarry. Bleed your brother, he said. You know, now that I think of it, maybe he thought I'd inherit the quarry or the money for it legally and he could collect all the Suriname money and whatever Sid got from the quarry if I was dead. Think maybe?"

"Maybe," I shrugged. "Maybe if Sid deposited the quarry money in the same account as your payoff money from Suriname. Why didn't you tell Sid who you were when you got back home?"

It was Georgia's turn to shrug. "I'd put in a little time in an ashram in India before I met Sid, so back in New York I joined up with the yoga center and loved it. Figured there was plenty of time. We'd be seeing each other in two years anyhow and, I mean, who's going to buy a slate quarry right off the bat? I see I should have come sooner and checked things out. Maybe talked to a slate lawyer or something. When you as much as said Gray was in Vermont I thought I could talk to him." She made a pistol of her hand and aimed at her temple. "Crazy me. Now I don't know what to think, but I can tell you I wish I was someplace else."

"Let's get out of here."

I held up a hand and Georgia pulled me to my feet.

There were no tools. I reasoned they must be in the garage. No lumber to whack at the door. One flimsy broom handle wouldn't do it.

Georgia braced herself on the top step and kicked the door,

but her sneaker bounced off the wood and she verbalized the pain.

"Oh!" I said. "Come here. Get down on your hands and knees. Georgia, we've found it!"

At the bottom of the furnace I had spotted a curved door held in place not by hinges but on gudgeons. It was about the size of a *National Geographic,* had a handle, and appeared to be cast iron.

Georgia grunted as she worked the door off the pins and grinned when she held her prize high. "This will do it."

I hadn't seen her smile before. It made me feel better. It also made me think that perhaps it would be a good idea just to hang out in the cellar and smile and let the cockeyed world get along without us.

Georgia assumed a balanced stance. "Here goes." She slammed the iron slab against one of the door panels and instead of the splintering sound I expected, the door opened and Georgia landed on her face on the kitchen floor.

Sophie was hopping around on one leg. "Oh my God, you broke my shin."

Georgia, now in a crouch, held her bloody hands to her face as we both watched Sophie.

"I'm sorry. So sorry."

"What did you hit me with—a fucking iron frying pan?"

By then I'd made it up the stairs. We all lowered the decibel level and I explained our situation. Sophie, holding a wet dish towel on her shin, said that she had driven back to Lofton and, finding no one, had come here. "I just turned the doorknob and started to slide the bolt when—when this happened."

No one drove by when we made our exit. Still hopping on one foot, Sophie held onto Georgia's arm. Georgia's other arm held mine in a strong grip. We must have looked like the defeated team being led from the line of scrimmage.

I was ready for home. No more trying to right the wrongs of the world for me. My plan was henceforth simply to stay in my studio and the hell with everyone else.

It even hurt when Lulu jumped in my lap. Her fuzzy black muzzle against my cheek made me feel teary with relief that I was really back home. A wreck, but home.

Hilary burst in through the door. A stalk of Brussels sprouts stuck out of his bag of groceries.

"Whew, you look like hell. Don't move a muscle. What you need is a drink."

To have Hilary lean over you is like being in the shadow of a giant derrick at a construction site. The Scotch he handed me wasn't just a couple of ounces of booze on ice with a splash of seltzer. It was heaven. I had yet to take a sip. It was the reassuring texture of my glass. Having had an almost terminal fright, plus shattering my knee again, to say nothing of crawling around on thorns and being locked in a cellar, it felt good to have something familiar—something that meant the end of the day—clutched in my hand.

Georgia emerged from the library bathroom looking much like my original impression of her—rather plain, with lovely blond hair and perfect yoga posture. Her long scratch was livid but no longer bleeding.

Hil looked at me with raised eyebrows.

"You haven't met?" I introduced Georgia to Hilary.

"The Georgia." Hilary shook her hand. "Greenwich Village Georgia? What's been going on around here? Fill me in."

"You tell him, Georgia," I said. "I want to hear if our day sounds as insane as I think it was."

Her precise rendition of events was so unemotional, she made the last five or six hours seem no more exciting than an afternoon at a mall.

I beckoned to Sophie while Georgia was still talking. "Where's Butler?" I whispered.

She assured me that Mrs. Butler had said her husband was on the way.

Gray had probably crossed the border by now, but somehow I didn't care. Abused is an overworked word, but that's the way I felt. Gray had taken advantage of me, of all of us, to say nothing of being a cold-blooded murderer. I didn't care whether Butler caught him or not. I wanted him to be erased. Somebody that never happened. Just a few lousy weeks in Vermont.

No one had time to greet Detective Butler when he barged in. I started right away with a rush of narrative. Didn't give the man a chance to say a word. "And believe it or not," I finished, "I remember Gray's license plate number."

"You can be sure we have that," he said.

I had tried to make up for not having recognized the Millers' blue car at Sophie's that day. "I want you to look at this." I held out the slide of Sid and the Indian. "Take it over to the light." Butler went over to the window and held up the slide. "Oh, here. This is for you." He turned and handed me a folded card.

"My glasses! Sophie, do you see them?"

Before Sophie plucked the card out of my hand, I saw dark smudges that had to be fingerprints. "Fingerprints! Hurry, child. I guess that will cinch the case."

"Yeah," she said. "It will. Says here, Tish, that the prints belong to Jake Miller!"

Hil said he'd be damned; Sophie said what do you know about that; Georgia repeated Jake's name. I had no comment.

Finally I spoke to Butler. "You knew before you saw the prints?"

"Miller was my number one suspect, and the fingerprints did it. Thanks to you. But if you'd asked me yesterday afternoon, I'd have told you the prints belonged to Mr. Gray. You see, the glass from Mr. Oats that you left at the station had Mr. Miller's prints on it which we took to be Gray's. Of course, we sent someone right off to get a set of Gray's prints off his doorknob. They will, of course, be routinely checked."

Even though I was numbed by the news about Jake, I did remember that first dinner at Hil's, being gratified to see that Gray knew how to pick up a wine glass, by the stem.

"Why did the Millers come back to Lofton?" Hilary asked. "Why didn't they keep going? You might never have caught up with them."

"Their accident was our lucky break, and the account they gave of just sort of deciding to come back, well, I can assure you they were carefully escorted back here. Jake claimed he had never been in your house, Mr. Oats, right?"

"No, not that I remember."

"From questioning Miller, it's become apparent that his wife, Wanda, really liked Sid Colt's attention, and that's what sent him over the edge. He said he doesn't remember hitting Colt. But there are those prints."

"Could he plead insanity?" Sophie asked.

"Could be." He shrugged.

"How about Graham Gray?" she asked. "He certainly turned out to be a bastard. Look what he did to Tish and Georgia."

Georgia turned her cheek for all to see, and I held up a chunk of my hair, brown with burrs.

"Will you try to catch him?" Georgia asked.

"I agree with Miss Beaumont that he's a bastard, but we have no evidence of any crime he's committed. There's the possibility of him pushing Mr. Oats into the quarry, but Mrs. Wyman called me to say both she and her husband knew it was an accident and begged me to take their word for it. The judgment there is yours, sir."

"I knew it was an accident," Hilary said. "But for interest's sake, what did happen?"

"To start with, Edgar Wyman says he'll never leave keys in a car or pickup again. The driver of one of those huge trucks had to turn the thing around to back into the pit. He moved the pickup out of the way. The driver said he thought he might have hit something, but there was nothing there."

"He was right," Hilary said. "I wasn't there. I was on a ledge hanging on for dear life. Let's forget it."

"Tish," Sophie said, "I know it was Vanessa's hair on Gray that got you thinking about him as the murderer, but you know, that blue sweater—he wore it a lot and I think he wore it that first night at Hil's so that's when he must have gotten Vanessa's hairs."

"Maybe."

"The proper authorities will be notified of Graham Gray's name change and his connection with the Nassau bank. I think you can take comfort in the fact that life could be made very unpleasant for him. If we've covered everything, I have to go."

"The picture, the slides," I said. I wasn't about to let Butler leave to go on doing whatever he did on his day off without telling me what he thought of the picture of Sid with his victim.

"Oh, yes. I'll hold onto this, Mrs. McWhinny, and we'll figure out its importance in the light of all the other events."

Incensed at the brush-off, with some effort I stood up. "You can't go yet. I mean, what did Jake say about the fingerprints? What did he do—just sit there and admit his guilt? For Pete's sake, tell us."

Hilary, using his Admiral-at-the-bridge voice, told Butler that he, too, was waiting to learn more about Jake.

The detective sighed and hooked his rear end on the window seat.

"Of course he denied the charge. He did admit that he went to your house, Mr. Oats. Said he'd collected some chanterelles for you. Went in to leave them in your kitchen, and since you weren't there, he called his wife to see if there was someone else who wanted them that he might have forgotten. Says there was no answer. So he went on back to the store."

Hilary frowned. "He went into my kitchen?"

"Yes. Said he was thirsty after picking the mushrooms. That's when he picked up the wine glass you brought us. Said he didn't see anyone. Not Sid, not Graham. Said he had nothing to do with the dynamite at your house, or your car. His fingerprints were on the telephone. Along with yours, Mrs. McWhinny."

"And on the pictures in Hilary's bedroom?" I asked.

"No, those were judged to be old or not relevant. Except for one or two on the very bottom that will be checked out."

We mumbled our goodbyes. I felt utterly deflated, said yes too easily when Hilary persuaded me to come with him into the kitchen.

"Sit," he commanded. "This won't hurt and it'll make you feel better."

Mercifully, there wasn't a mirror in the kitchen, so I couldn't watch Hilary cutting the burrs out of my hair. It did make me feel better. But not much.

TWENTY-TWO

Georgia pleaded, begged us, not to question her. Tomorrow, she said. "Tomorrow, I hope I will have regained my sanity. Just let me go to bed. And thanks for letting me stay, Mrs. McWhinny."

Sophie looked drawn and dazed and barely said goodnight before she went upstairs and collapsed in the guest room opposite Georgia's.

Hilary had gone home with no urging, but not before he had assured Georgia that he'd be back in the morning to hear the whole story.

I knew I couldn't sleep. The only reason I went to bed was sheer exhaustion. Lulu gets the worst of it when I toss and turn. She wriggles around, trying to dodge my elbows and knees.

Branches were banging on my bathroom window, and I decided to get up and go out to the shed, retrieve the long-handled pruner, and cut the darn things off. I'd been meaning to do it for weeks. But I didn't pursue my foolish idea because I was diverted by the sight of a car without lights moving slowly along

Main Street. It came to a stop beside the church. It was too dark to see if anyone emerged, so I tiptoed out into the hall and stood at the top of the stairs listening to the night noises.

Soon I heard it. It was only a slight sound, but I knew it was the back doorknob moving. It always sounded as though it was embedded in peanut brittle.

I didn't wait to hear more. I flew into Sophie's room, grabbing Lulu in flight. Inside, I shoved her under Sophie's covers. Sophie shot up in alarm, and we cracked heads with such ferocity that it brought tears to my eyes. I put my hand over her mouth. "Shhhh," I whispered. "Someone just came into the house."

Naked, she slithered out of bed and grabbed her shorts and her Jurassic Park T-shirt and tiptoed over to the closed door. Then she sank to her hands and knees, and with her fanny in the air like a puppy ready to play she peeked through the crack under the door. I joined her on my belly.

Whoever was creeping around downstairs was bigger than I, and probably a lot tougher than Sophie, though most prowlers might think twice about tackling her. I don't want you to think she's brawny or looks like a weightlifter. Not at all. She's lovely and lithe; but there is something about her level gaze and her way of placing her hands on her hips that doesn't invite contradiction.

I grabbed her arm as she reached for the doorknob. "No."

"Yes," she whispered. "I'll go see who it is."

"NO, NO, NO." I can look fierce, too, and Sophie resumed her previous pose.

I thought of all the possible escape routes. The choice was between jumping a whole story and ending up in the hospital or the morgue, or a hanging descent from the porch roof. Its surface was metal and now covered with leaves. It would make a child's slide seem slow.

There was no telephone in either guest room. But what good would that do? Who would I call? Damned if I'd bother Hilary. There was a light upstairs in the store. Wanda must be there, or maybe she had been taken to Rutland along with Jake.

"I'll bet it's Gray," I whispered. "Changed his mind and wants Georgia to go with him."

"Or wants to kill her. I tell you, Tish, she's scared."

Sophie had risen to open the closet door. She took out a ski pole. Next, she handed me a short-handled fishing net, or was it something for jai-alai or maybe lacrosse? I'd rarely poked around in Doug's hideaway for sports gear. I failed to see that whatever it was could be any help.

We both heard the sound of scratching on Georgia's door. Sophie slid to the floor again. "Maybe he's trying to wake her up. Hope she locked the door."

The scratching was not a sound that would ever wake a Vermonter up—at least, not this one. Most of us are accustomed to the noisy bands of field mice working, playing, mating, holding up most of our walls—rather like insulation in motion.

"Listen, Tish. When he wakes her up, the minute he goes into the room, bang on her door, hard, and jump back in here and lock your door." She moved over to the window. "Maybe they'll try to go out the window and I'll be out on the roof with this." She gripped the ski pole. "Where's your gun?"

"If that's Gray, he has it."

"Shit. Well, whoever it is, I'll knock them off the roof. It's not very high, won't hurt them. Hey look." She pointed to a gallon can. "I'll pour this over them."

Improbable as it seemed under the circumstances, I had to

smile. The ghostly vision of Georgia and Gray covered with whitewash pleased me.

Sophie's bedroom had a small brick whitewashed fireplace, and I remembered admonishing myself for being a slob and leaving the can upstairs when I gave its façade its most recent coat. I crawled over and stirred the paint with the handle of the other ski pole. An unlikely brew for a witch, but satisfying.

Doug had always been on the verge of putting up a swing. Loops of various-sized ropes hung from hooks in the closet. I reached for the rope I thought of as mine. Thanks to a youthful summer in Montana, I fancied myself as a rope twirler, so Doug had fashioned a wee noose at one end of the line, thus creating a lariat for me.

Sophie gave me the thumbs-up, and crawled through the window. The dinosaur on her chest was swallowed by the night.

With the lariat over my shoulder, I pressed my ear to the door. Silence. I inhaled as I turned the knob and peeked out into the hall. I had no intention of obeying Sophie. If they went out onto the porch roof as she expected, then I'd follow her out there. If they went down the hall and downstairs, I'd make for an exit too—all with the asinine hope of lassoing somebody.

My course of action was decided by a wild ruckus on the roof. I tore downstairs with my bathrobe flying behind me. I nearly went through the screen door before I could unhook it. Standing stock still on the porch, I witnessed an orgiastic scene beyond belief. Gray, Georgia, and Sophie were writhing like serpents on my token front yard. Sophie looked like the Brunhilde of octopuses. Yelling her head off, she seemed to en-velope the other two. If she had added whitewash to the mix they would have looked like squirming termites or maybe the Laocoön.

My neighbor Katie ran out of her house wearing a pink chenille robe and an old-fashioned nightcap, and lugging a blunderbuss her husband had used in the Mexican War.

Wanda, fully dressed, came running across the street and aimed a powerful flashlight on the undulating mass.

I don't know how long we watched helplessly. Then Gray seemed to slip away from Sophie's grasp. Georgia hastily pushed one of her ample breasts back into her torn T-shirt. The moment had come for me to act and I did so by stepping back a pace. I need space and a straight arm to get my rope to form into a proper circle. In seconds, Gray's head popped up in the right spot and presented the perfect target for my skill. I could hear everyone gasp (we had quite a crowd by then) as the loop encircled Gray's head. Quickly I pulled the lariat taut. Gray gurgled, and the audience exhaled.

Gray's attempt to grab the rope only tightened the noose. Sophie knelt on his chest.

"Okay, Gray, let's hear it. Give him a little slack, Tish. He's going to tell us why he was in your house. Right, Gray?"

He gurgled. I gave him more slack.

"I came," he said, "to get Georgia."

"Yeah." Sophie tweaked the rope. "And that's why you locked her in your cellar this afternoon, right?"

Katie moved in closer. Her obvious enthusiasm for the fray made me wonder if she'd had a bedtime sip of pumpkin liquor. "You—" She poked Georgia in the back with the gun. "Were you going away with that man?"

"No, no. Not willingly. He's got a gun."

With that news, a wild wrestling match began. I loosened my hold on the rope. I was afraid I might crush Gray's larynx.

Sophie had managed to turn around, and now straddled Gray

with her rump in his face and her hands reaching for the gun.

Charlie, in jeans and pajama tops, caught one of Gray's hands in both of his, and Wanda stood with both feet planted on his other wrist and hand.

Sophie had unzipped Gray's fly, but still no sign of my gun.

"I've got it." Georgia withdrew her arm from under thoroughly beaten Gray and waved the gun overhead. Sophie then slid down and sat on his legs.

"Let the poor guy get up."

I don't know who said that, but none of the four of us budged.

Sophie, looking wild-eyed, went well with the dinosaur on her shirt, and she wasn't about to move. Tiny Kate was a memorable sight, standing firm with her gigantic weapon. Wanda looked tight-lipped and ferocious. Georgia, with my gun in her hand, looked calm and resolute. The livid scar running down her face must have sent a message to the onlookers that this was no game. She had a lot more gumption than I would have guessed. Maybe Gray's defenseless state squared her shoulders—or perhaps my gun. I remembered the fleeting sense of power it had given me.

And me, barefoot, in a short white nightie that showed under my untied white velour robe. The aged avenging angel, all in white. And I wasn't about to let go of my lasso.

A fleeting pang of sympathy made me think that tidy Gray would hate the way he looked right now. Neither Charlie nor Wanda had released his hands, and no one had bothered to zip him up. A casual observer might think we'd caught a rapist.

"This man, this creep,"—Georgia had our attention—"would have killed me today if it hadn't been for Mrs. McWhinny coming to the quarry."

"That's ridiculous," Gray croaked.

"This man wanted not only the money he killed Sid to get, but he wanted my share of our money."

"That's ridiculous."

"This man thought he could get away with murder, too." Georgia was no longer calm. She waved the gun again. Her mouth worked like a llama about to spit.

Sophie reached out her long arm and yanked the rope out of my hands. She jerked Gray as though he were a dog being trained on a choke collar.

"Let's hear it from you, you murderer." She jerked again.

"You'll kill him, Sophie," Charlie warned. "Someone's called the police. Better wait."

A voice asked, "Is he the fellow that killed Sid Colt?"

What a vision I must have been as I raised my hand for silence. "I don't think he'll tell us. Let's hear it from you, Georgia. Do you really know that he murdered Sid?"

In silence we listened to the wind before Georgia spoke. "Sure he murdered Sid. Strong, silent Gray. Pretended to be my friend. Ha-ha. Figured he'd go off to Nassau and collect all the money. Our money, Sid's money. But after you locked us in the cellar and left you began thinking, didn't you. Gosh—maybe someone else knew I was Sid's stepsister and maybe I was Sid's heir to the quarry. Right, Gray? So you came back to kill me. Right? Then guess what." She looked at her audience. "The greedy pig would take all the money and disappear from the face of the earth. You pig." She kicked the sole of his shoes.

"Can you prove what you're saying?" My Lord, that was Hilary asking the question. Someone must have called him. We looked at each other. My grateful look must have felt like a hug.

Georgia wasn't finished. "You're going to confess, aren't you, Gray, Greg, or whatever your real name is." The angry woman then demonstrated her yogic agility and strength and fell into Sophie's original position, straddling Gray's skinny chest. Leaning over almost nose-to-nose, she placed her thumbs on either side of his eyes. "Remember? Sid told us how to do this. Tell them, Gray. Tell them you killed Sid."

"Yes, yes. Oh, God, yes! Get her off me!" Gray wrenched his arms free. But whatever Georgia had done must have put mortal fear in the man. He was limp, and repeated, "Yes, yes, I killed him."

Georgia sat back, her face whiter than ever. Gray seemed intact. We all sighed with relief that Georgia hadn't gouged out his eyes, if that was her intent. Maybe she'd mesmerized him with some weird trick—maybe pressure on certain nerves.

Charlie pulled him into a sitting position, and someone took the noose off his head.

Just why Charlie helped up Gray I wouldn't know. Everyone must have been mightily confused by what Georgia had said, and I guess since it seemed to have established that Gray was the murderer, the unusual drama was over. Time for a little relaxing intermission before the police came.

I leaned over to pick up the rope that had been carelessly tossed on the grass—when it happened.

The pain was like a white-hot dagger in my shoulder. I screamed. Gray had grabbed my hand in the oldest, scariest trick of all. He folded my arm behind my back and pulled my hand up to my shoulder blade.

Gray didn't have to raise his voice when he spoke to the others. Everyone heard him. Even the wind seemed to cease for a minute. I could feel his breath on the top of my head.

"You all know, and Tish knows, that I can break her arm, dislocate her shoulder, and toss her over that stone wall for scrap.

I suggest you all back away. You, too, lady." He looked at dangerous little Katie. "Put that gun down."

She hesitated.

"Put it down, Kate, please." My voice didn't sound commanding. I was pleading.

She lowered the barrel a foot. "You sure, Tish? I don't mind shooting him."

"Please, Katie, put it down."

Charlie stepped over and took the gun out of her hands, sliding it onto the porch.

Gray jerked my arm. "We're taking your car. You're driving."

In the dark? Without my glasses? I knew I'd never even leave Lofton alive, and we'd probably both be killed.

"Listen, Greg. If you move one inch, a half an inch, I'm going to empty this gun at you. I'm gonna kill you." Georgia stood off to one side with my pistol aimed at Gray. He turned his head to look at her.

Then, thank goodness, I heard Hilary's voice. I knew when he told Gray not to move that he was in charge. He had lifted Kate's gun off the porch and its three-foot barrel was aimed at Gray's midsection. "Sorry, Tish. Hope I don't have to splatter him all over you." If Hilary pulled the trigger Gray and I would both be in confetti-sized pieces. I held my breath. Hilary moved a few steps closer. "It's not quite clear to me, but you're going to tell me why you killed Sid."

Even in the closeness of our miserable embrace I could barely hear Gray's voice. "He had no intention of keeping an agreement we had made."

"An agreement?" I was surprised to hear my own strong voice.

Georgia moved closer. "What agreement?"

"In return for me engineering the rice deal in Suriname we

both signed a contract that promised me a third of the money he'd get when he sold the quarry."

Georgia's hiss sounded reptilian.

"Then he tore it, right in front of my face, he tore it into pieces. We argued, he pushed me, I pushed him and he fell. I knew he could break me in two so I hit him."

"With the poker?"

"With the poker. I didn't mean to kill him. It was an accident."

"You're supposed to report an accident," Sophie said acidly. "You let us go to Hilary's house knowing Sid was there—dead!"

Gray avoided her eyes by lowering his head.

"Sid," said Hilary, "was taking care of my cat. Why were *you* in my house?"

"I was in the post office and saw Sid walking up your road. You were in the hospital. I wanted to talk to him."

Gray had loosened his hold on me and I began inching away. Thank goodness others, led by Charlie, took charge of Gray. Sophie put a long strong arm around me and almost carried me up the stairs and into the house. Lulu was frantic with relief that the noisy scene outside was over, and ran between Sophie and Hilary and me to make sure we were intact. When Georgia came in and sank into one end of the couch she gave her a fuzzy kiss, too.

"Wow, you were really cool," Sophie said to Georgia.

Sophie's word "cool" wasn't one I would have used to describe Georgia's torrid yet steely performance just now. But it made it easier to imagine her making her way through a barricade of legalities to the ultimate pot of gold. After all, if Uncle Slate had known about her existence she might have been the one to inherit the quarry.

"I think we can all believe Gray. Right, Tish? He did it. Fini, goodbye to the bad actor."

"You mean a good actor. He fooled me," I said. "But I guess like everything else about me, my judgment is deteriorating."

"He fooled all of us, Tish," Hilary said. "I apologize for bringing the man into our lives."

Sophie jumped to her feet and dashed into the library. We could hear her swearing, and then the rat-tat-tat of my old typewriter.

We listened in silence till she reappeared, waving a paper overhead. "A confession, a signed confession, is what we need."

"Great idea." Georgia jumped up. "I'll help you."

"Nope, you stay here. You've done your part. We don't want the police to say his confession was forced."

There was skepticism in our voices as Hilary and I wished Sophie good luck in unison. Wild horses couldn't have dragged me outside again, but we watched from the windows.

Gray was standing with his back against my car. Charlie, grim-faced, held my little pistol against his ribs.

I never thought I could be glad to see Turk Smith at such close range. The brute was fully dressed, and I guessed he must have been driving through Lofton when the ruckus started. He held Gray's elbow in his beefy grip. I could see Sophie's back, with her hands on her hips. Wanda, who had joined her, was gesticulating. I could see the top of Gray's head, so I guessed his chin was on his chest. I felt sure they were getting nowhere. Why would they? Gray had done and said enough for one day.

Everyone turned at the sight of the police car lights and watched a uniformed officer emerge and walk toward them.

I couldn't look any longer. I knew, without waiting for Butler's proof, that Gray's prints would be identified as those on the bottom of the frame. And that Georgia, because of getting Gray's confession by force, would probably testify about his dishonorable past.

Looking tired and dejected, Sophie limped in and sank on the couch and hugged Lulu.

"No luck." She tore up the unsigned confession. "Guess Detective Butler struck out. But at least we can leave all the sorting and fingerprinting to him. You must be a wreck, Tish. How come you get involved in all these nutty things?"

I had no answer to that question.

"Damn that Gray." Sophie stretched. "Damn, damn, damn. What's the matter with me, Tish? All these damn no-good guys I get mixed up with."

It's true. Sophie hadn't had a good guy since that cute reporter two years ago. There were slim pickings in Lofton and the imports had indeed been poor quality lately.

"When will it be over? How long does it take, Tish, to get beyond all this?"

"All what?"

"You know—. Men, sex."

"I don't know, dear. You'll have to ask someone older than I."

Sophie laughed. "Guess I'll have to ask Hilary."

"You do that."

She rose and stretched; she clasped her hands behind her back and bent over to rest her forehead against her knees.

Georgia slithered to the carpet, and, lying on her back, raised straight legs in the air and lifted her arms and held on to her toes. I joined them. Minutes later, I caught sight of Hilary, who had gone into the kitchen to make cocoa for us. With Lulu tucked under one arm, he stood in the doorway smiling at the sight of all three of us standing on our heads.